COLLEEN J. PALLAMARY

The Vampire Preservation Society

by

Colleen J. Pallamary

Pallamary Publishing

COLLEEN J. PALLAMARY

THE VAMPIRE PRESERVATION SOCIETY

Pallamary Publishing
Ocala, FL
www.pallamarypublishing.com

First published by Pallamary Publishing January 19, 2015

ISBN 10: 0692341463 (sc)
ISBN 13: 978-0692341469 (sc)
Printed in the United States of America
North Charleston, South Carolina

This book is printed on acid-free paper made from 30% post-consumer waste recycled material.

Library of Congress Control Number: 2014921481

Book Jacket and Page Design: Matthew J. Pallamary/San Diego CA
Cover Art: Lane Erickson - Dreamstime

In Loving Memory of My Mom Colleen J. Kennedy

Here's Uncle Don, with the winners, Colleen Bartram and Gary Coles (real name Anthony de Couci) of New Haven. Gary is 12, and sings "sophisticated songs" like *Down Argentine Way*. The finals were held in the old New Amsterdam Theater, where Ziegfeld used to run his Follies. The two winners will start for Hollywood May 4, stopping over to see Mayor Kelly of Chicago, and then to see the Grand Canyon of the Colorado. Their trip will take three weeks in all, including visits to the Hollywood studios. One of last year's winners, Buddy Swalm, who did Orson Welles imitations in a beard, is now the Buddy Swan of the cast of *Citizen Kane*, playing Charles Foster Kane (Orson Welles) as a boy of 8.

COLLEEN J. PALLAMARY

"Don't be afraid little girl. I won't hurt you. This is all make-believe."

Bela Lugosi to my Mom, age 10. Hollywood, CA.

COLLEEN J. PALLAMARY

ACKNOWLEDGEMENTS

The Vampire Preservation Society is a tale of survival fueled by the ageless bonds of friendship, love, and forgiveness. Originally a short story tucked away in more places than I can count, *The Vampire Preservation Society* resurfaced many times over the last twenty years haunting the writer inside of me who hid behind a wall of doubt. At last I am ready to share the immortal world I created devoid of gratuitous violence and glistening gore. Escape for a while and spend some time with immortal characters whose worldviews may be closer to yours than you think.

I would like to thank my brother and fellow author, Matthew J. Pallamary, for his support and encouragement; Maryellen Rivers and Rita Knopf for sticking with me through the various story incarnations; Lynne Engel-Holmes and her daughters Crystal and Rachael Holmes for their valuable input and assistance; Santa Barbara Writer's Conference and Southern California Writer's Conference for their excellent programs, leaders, and instructors.

Much gratitude and love to my children Michelle, MaryAnne, and Carl for listening to their Mom ramble on about vampires for so many years. To my grandchildren Cody, Kayla, Stevie, and Nik – you are my sunshine and my world. I love you all very much!

Last but not least, much love and misses to those cherished people who have passed on but still live in my heart. Thanks Mom, Auntie Pip, Tony, Carl, Rita, and Sue for accepting and loving me unconditionally and for visiting me in my dreams. You are each immortal in your own way!

CHAPTER ONE

A cool breeze rustled the golden leaves of a sugar maple tree as the waxing gibbous moon began its ascent into a star-speckled sky. Branford Winston smiled and brushed unruly coffee colored curls out of his eyes as he sauntered towards the state line of Massachusetts. The young vampire was on his way to the annual Vampire Preservation Society meeting and could hardly wait to see old friends, share new adventures, and sample the local cuisine. Soon the ocean breeze would tickle his nose and whet his appetite for a piece of briny New England mortal.

The unmistakable stench of an unwashed human drifted through the air and Branford paused to investigate. A young man huddled in a vacant storefront doorway mumbled something about the Mayan calendar and UFOs between sips of cheap wine and tokes on a skinny joint. Not one to pass up an easy meal, Branford sidled up to the shivering vagrant and whispered into his ear. "You've found your UFO. I'm an Unidentified Feral Object and you can mark this day as your last on the calendar of your choice."

The kill was quick and warm blood filled his belly like a hot cup of tea. He wiped his lips with the back of his hand and a piercing pain shot through his jaw and into both fangs. Reaching into his mouth to massage aching gums, he was shocked when both incisors popped out and tumbled to the ground coming to rest in a patch of dried weeds. "What the hell!" he shrieked. "Baby fangs? Am I teething like a mortal or is this from not brushing after every meal? Cut the shit! How do I get new ones?"

The baffled vampire bent over to retrieve his razor sharp teeth and fell forward hitting his head on the cold asphalt and scraping his knees like a child at play. Foul fluids dribbled out of the sides of his mouth and his vision dimmed while jumbled images of his rebirth played in his mind like an old black and white film from the silent era: the flames of his campfire at his hunting ground near Hudson Bay, early 1800's; soft animal pelts sliding between the thick fingers of his roughened hands; snow crunching beneath his ear; being shoved to the ground by a mysterious stranger whispering a cryptic greeting near his frozen beard; warm blood trickling down his buckskin jacket as two icy incisors slashed the tender skin of his neck; and finally, a cold metal ring placed on a limp finger twitching in the snow.

Searing pain in both ears jolted Branford back to the present. Dampness seeped into his aching skull and his eyelids fluttered as he watched a swirling mist dance around the golden streetlamp overhead. The need for sleep was overwhelming. Red neon lights flashing *2015 Blood Drive* on an old movie marquee beckoned like a cozy coffin on a raw winter day. The bruised immortal crawled towards an alley beside the old theatre but never made it to the comforting light. He closed his fluttering eyelids and listened to the screeching cries of a wild animal echoing through the quiet streets, soon realizing that the frantic screams were his own. Within seconds his trembling body disintegrated into a pile of cobalt blue ash and his copper ring skittered across the asphalt and came to rest beside a crumpled Dunkin Donuts coffee cup.

Branford Winston, immortal fur trapper and valued community member, was dead at the young age of 200. Cause of death unknown.

CHAPTER TWO

The annual Vampire Preservation Society meeting was the most anticipated event of the year. Members from around the world converged at a chosen location to celebrate, socialize, and conduct seminars on survival and ritual techniques. The 2014 meeting was being held in Gloucester, Massachusetts, a small fishing village hugging the coast of New England. The proximity to Salem, home of the infamous Salem witches, played a role in providing a safe environment for immortals who wanted to explore the area in an inconspicuous manner. Individuality and metaphysics were the norm in the tiny town and eccentricities were encouraged and welcomed by all.

Vampiric travel was somewhat diverse. Contrary to popular belief, immortals did not shapeshift into bats or other supernatural forms. Some preferred the mundane mortal modes of transportation as a way to keep on top of current trends, share information about hunting grounds, or as a way to battle boredom. Others chose a quick and efficient method of roving known as *vamporization*, a technique that accelerated the vibrational rate of their bodies until they dissolved into puffs of glittering white dust. Materialization was a simple matter of melding the twinkling particles together until they returned to solid form. Adventurous vampires tried mingling with snowflakes and tumbled to the ground before resuming form and ethereal daredevils rode turbulent storm clouds, twisting and turning in chaotic free-fall until deciding where to land. Occasionally a neophyte vamp forgot to take time zones into consideration and ended up evaporating in blazing sunlight like a raindrop plopping on a sizzling grill. Similar to other sentient creatures, travel was a matter of preference and convenience.

The meeting night had finally arrived. Laughter drifted through the cool, pine-scented air as excited guests strolled along a winding cobblestone path leading to the castle home of vampire leader Lucien LaPierre, a wealthy art dealer of European descent. An ornate wrought-iron gate guarded the entrance to the fortress known as Nightshade Manor and it served several purposes. Before entering the grounds each vampire held his or her sacred copper ring up to a scanner which downloaded encrypted information into a small chip embedded into the tumblers of a stainless steel lock. If approved, the gate swung open and a burly immortal bouncer called "Harker the Barker" scrutinized each member as they passed through to the celebration, a secondary precaution used to detect any intruders of the mortal persuasion. Attendance at the annual summer solstice meeting was mandatory for many of the attendees and the digital ring-reading system doubled as a census device to help ensure survival of the species.

Conventions were gala affairs celebrating the nuances of immortality. Members dressed in a variety of fashions ranging from re-birth suits (clothing from the era when they had become immortal) to antique costumes handed down from one generation to the next. The newest undead donned many of the fickle mortal fashions that changed with each passing season and more practiced members wore whatever combinations pleased them from several different eras. Refreshments were always a delight. Favorites included bloodsicles, a frozen delicacy imported from clandestine locations scattered across the world and Hemosip, an organic concoction of freshly squeezed blood from several warm-blooded sources. Excited guests hugged and toasted each other while waiting for the meeting to begin.

CHAPTER THREE

Jade Lee, the petite Asian vampire leader, clutched a large manila envelope in one hand and a copy of her latest best-selling mystery novel *Night Bites* in the other. Her long blue-black hair cascaded down her back in a perfect v-shaped formation and two hair combs embedded with emeralds and pearls accented her green almond shaped eyes and pale snowy skin. It was her idea to have a pre-party meeting with the others to discuss the dwindling census numbers she had discovered earlier that week. She was also slated to give a presentation on her experiences as an immortal author masquerading as a mortal in the cut-throat world of publishing and wanted to review her notes.

At the end of a long candlelit hallway she reached for a large metal ring embedded in a huge oak door and pulled the meeting room door open. Orange flames from a crackling fireplace spit warmth into the chilly room and painted muted shadows on the silvery stone walls. Nightshade Manor was one of her favorite places to visit and she curled up on a small brocaded settee to wait for the others with the familiarity of one who feels at home and stared into the flames remembering her rebirth.

Re-born during the California Gold Rush after she and her

parents fled China during the Taiping Rebellion, Jade Lee hoped for a new life free of oppression and fear. They borrowed money from an underground broker in Hong Kong with a promise to repay in full once they "struck it rich" in the land of *gum saan,* or "gold mountain" as it was known in China. Passage was booked on a laundry ship returning clean shirts and linens to rugged miners who refused to wash their own filthy clothing and chose to send it overseas rather than deal with the unsavory chore themselves. After several weeks on a crowded, creaking ship the weary family disembarked in San Francisco, a raucous settlement where prospectors and prostitutes all hoped to benefit from the legendary Mother Lode of glittering gold.

The ambitious Lee family opened their own business shortly after landing. *Feng Shui Laundry* sat on a small hill near the water and offered easy access to those in need of wardrobe washing. Boisterous crews gathered sweat-stained shirts and muddy trousers for drop-off and returned later in the week to pick up their freshly pressed attire. One day a disheartened gold digger traded his new journal, jar of ink, and tattered quill for a few clean shirts and Jade tucked it away in a safe place to use during the rare moments when she was alone.

The gray days and damp nights of the "City by the Bay" seemed endless. Scraping smelly fabric on a washboard in cold, murky water made the young woman feel as dirty and grimy as the street urchins lurking behind barrels and rickety buildings scattered around the dusty town. Late one evening, while sitting on a rock outside the laundry facing the bay, Jade heard the booming voices of drunken men singing one of their now familiar racist tunes.

"Coolie, Coolie one, two, three, come on out and clean for me, Coolie Coolie four, five, six, we'll whack you hard with muddy picks."

The word "coolie", a derogatory term for Chinese immigrants, didn't bother her as much as the veiled threats to her family and friends. Ignorant fools always lose she thought, watching them stagger and stumble between shabby canvas tents and waning campfires. Jade missed China and longed for the old way of life when people worked together and respected each other, the exact opposite of what she and her family were experiencing here. She leaned back on a weather-beaten tree stump and began to cry. The earth beneath her tiny feet rumbled and she felt, rather than heard, a deep voice resonating in her head.

"I am the answer to your pain and troubles. I can lead you to everlasting life and love."

Startled, Jade looked behind her and saw a figure nestled in the shadows of an old dilapidated shack not far from the family business. "We are impressed with you, young one, for honoring your family and helping others in this foreign land. Your kindness and eagerness to learn have captured our attention and we wish to reward you with the gift of eternal life."

A hint of warm air, like the tap of butterfly wings on a windowpane, brushed her eyelashes and grazed the tip of her upturned nose. Someone or something gently pulled her head back exposing the tender white skin and mottled blue veins of her delicate neck. A gentle hiss, like the sound of spit on a hot iron, was followed by a moment of prickling pain. A small ring was placed on her right hand and a gush of warmth washed through her toasting her chilled bones.

"There are obstacles to overcome, goals to be met, and precautions to take and you will persevere. Cloak yourself in the darkness of night and feed on the blood of living things until their hearts no longer beat. You are immortal now. Go forth as a leader. There are others and you will meet them when the time is right."

Jade's green eyes fluttered like two small emeralds floating in a pool of ice cold milk. The shadow figure grasped her slender ankles and dragged her to a copse of fragrant pine trees at the base of the hill. She tried to speak but only managed a low moan and in the stillness of the rising dawn her soul sank into oblivion.

CHAPTER FOUR

W olf Who Waits, Native American medicine man turned vampire leader, had just finished identifying and returning the skeletal remains of a long-deceased tribal member whose remains were unearthed near a creek in Northern California. As a consultant with NAGPRA, the Native American Graves Protection and Repatriation Act, it was his responsibility to return any remains and artifacts to their proper place for burial in accordance with the tribal customs of the deceased. His expertise in the field was one of the distinct advantages of immortality. Having lived in several eras Wolf was familiar with the ancestors of Native people. Repatriating their bodies and belongings was an honor.

He passed his copper ring through the gate sensor and made his way through a crowd of jubilant partygoers, nodding at Harker the Barker as he went by. He headed inside, soft moccasins skimming the cold stone floors until he reached the huge oak door of the meeting room. His regional census numbers were down and, more important, his discovery last week of a copper ring buried beneath a pile of cobalt blue ash was a cause for concern. He had carefully scooped up the remains and placed them in a small calfskin pouch that now hung from his neck beside a beaded medicine bag filled with sage and other sacred objects. Rather than disrupt the preparations and planning for the big party, he decided to wait and share his findings when the four leaders were all together.

Reunions always made vampires nostalgic. Some longed for centuries past when life was easier and feeding wasn't such a bore. Others, like Wolf, honored the memory of their own re-births by reliving the moments before the change. He could still smell the sweetgrass and cedar in his mind.

Wolf Who Waits, a Plains Indian, was re-born a few years before Jade, in the mid 1830's. Handsome and humble, with high cheekbones, eyes the color of warm amber honey, and coal black hair worn in a single thick braid, the young man had worked tirelessly with the Elders of many tribes to help heal their people's spiritual wounds. It was a turbulent time for Native American Indians across the land. President Andrew Jackson had signed the Indian Removal Act into law forcing tens of thousands of indigenous people to leave their native lands in the South for unknown territories in the West. Mandatory marches killed thousands of men, women, and children and left others to fend for themselves with rotted rationed food and tattered clothing distributed by callous military personnel. White settlers were intent on fulfilling their vision of Manifest Destiny at any cost, including the deaths of innocent people and destruction of their lands under the pretense of progress.

Meanwhile, to the North, pale strangers carried germ-laden blankets and clothing into Native villages and spread smallpox throughout the Plains tribes. Death tiptoed in silent footsteps and hid in the echoes of whispering winds. Frightened people looked to tribal leaders for guidance and Wolf consulted the Elders before deciding on his next step, a vision quest that would help him find a path to follow and the wisdom to walk that path towards healing the Native nations. After the purification of a sweat lodge ceremony he set out to find his special spot.

Wolf felt energized in the crumpled green quilt of Ponderosa pines and juniper trees thriving in the sacred Black

Hills of South Dakota. He lit a small fire, tossed pieces of dried cedar and white sage on the flames, and inhaled the fragrant smoke while it washed over his muscular body. A full moon poked its shiny bald head over a distant mountaintop and began to rise into the violet-blue sky. It was time to honor the four directions. Wolf stood and opened a deerskin pouch resting on his hip.

"Great Spirit of the East, my gift to you is snakeskin to show that we are always changing and growing in order to survive. Please hear my prayers." The crinkly, thin flesh floated softly to the eastern side of the circle.

"Spirit of the South, I offer the teeth of brother wolf so that we always remember the spirit of family and the gift of solitude when we need to pray. Please hear my prayers and give our people the will to live." He placed the teeth on a smooth stone facing the South.

"Spirit of the West, I give you my bear claw so that we may sit quietly and heed your words of advice. Please give us patience and hear my prayers." The bear claw curled around a pebble on the western section of warmed stones.

"Spirit of the North, please hear my prayers and accept my gift of an eagle feather so that our people can rise above their suffering and have a new beginning." He bent and placed the offering on the northern side of the circle.

A small gust of wind fanned the flames and a coyote howled in the distance. Wisps of smoke and glowing embers swirled in a spiral and a husky voice mingled with the sound of rustling leaves. "I hear your call and feel your need to help our relatives. I am here to answer your prayers and show you the way."

Wolf glanced up and saw a tall stranger dressed in soft fringed buckskin and a long buffalo robe worn fur side out, the traditional way of a warrior protecting loved ones. The young medicine man stared, unsure of how to react. The spirits had never shown themselves like this before.

"Smoke from the sacred pipe and hear what I offer. Our people are on the brink of extinction and we need strong leaders to help them survive."

Wolf sucked the smoke into his lungs and passed the pipe back to the stranger. "What can I do to help?" he asked.

"I have the gift of eternal life, my son," the man continued. "The stars and moon will be your allies and the darkness your greatest friend. Are you willing to accept your place among our people, to guide and protect them? It is a sacrifice to be sure, but your powers will be extraordinary and your name will become legendary in the stories we share with our children and grandchildren."

Wolf knew in his heart that he couldn't refuse. He looked into the iridescent eyes of the spirit-man and nodded yes, flying backwards as the buffalo robe enveloped him and the stranger's lips became a fang-filled grin. The stars overhead swayed in his vision and a sharp pain, like the prick of slender bone needles, pierced his neck and trickled down through his body till it reached his clenched bare toes. A small copper ring encircled his finger and he sank to the ground in a dreamless heap of immortality.

THE VAMPIRE PRESERVATION SOCIETY

CHAPTER FIVE

Jade jumped up and hugged Wolf when he entered the meeting room. They shared a history of sorts, both mortal and immortal, and enjoyed each other's company. "Good to see you brother," she whispered in his ear. He smiled and kissed her cheek.

"Still waiting on Savanna I see," he said.

"She's on her way. Lucien is out mingling with the minions and I am looking over some notes. I've got a few things to add to our agenda. I hope she gets here soon."

Savanna Martin, award-winning architect and graphic designer, was stuck in traffic on Route 1A trying to get to the meeting. Her short nutmeg hair, mocha skin, and doe-like cocoa eyes caught the eye of many a mortal and immortal admirer. Tonight was no exception. A tall traffic cop had informed her that a large oak tree had fallen across the road, blocking traffic in both directions. She had no choice but to wait for chainsaws and cutters to chip away at the mangled mess.

He reluctantly left after a few minutes of flirting, trying to get her phone number, and offering her a drink after he got off work. She had respectfully declined. No sense getting the local law upset. She checked her watch for the third time in as many minutes. Vamporization was not an option in this situation. She didn't want to leave her project materials behind or run the risk of having her Candy Apple Red 1968 Shelby Mustang Cobra GT 500KR towed and scratched by a moronic human bottom feeder with no appreciation for classic cars. She had decided at the last minute to take Sweetness, her pet name for her car, out for one last spin before the winter season forced her to store the cherished vehicle in a secured garage to avoid the salted roads and harsh winter weather that would damage the pristine body.

Resigned to spending some time in her antique vehicle, she traced the Cobra emblem on the polished dash with slender fingers then cradled a small carved sandalwood box in both hands. It contained five copper rings and a quart-sized baggie of cobalt blue ash. Vivid memories of her mortal life played in her head like the chattering lovebirds and parakeets of her homeland near the Gold Coast of West Africa.

Growing up Africa in the mid 1730's, Savanna was well-aware of the constant threat from poachers terrorizing villages and stealing people in the middle of the night to be sold as slaves to the settlers in the British Colonies of America. Strong young men who otherwise would be guarding their families were taken first and defenseless women and children were left to devise their own strategies for survival.

From a young age Savanna delighted in drawing shapes and designs in the moist jungle soil. The lines and ridges of geometric patterns were carefully crafted with sticks and pebbles and the more she drew the better her skills. Her creative nature was instrumental in hiding many members of her tribe from the marauders who believed money was more important than morals and was a precursor to her work with the Underground Railroad a century later. Small furrows covered in palm fronds and leaves dotted the outskirts of her village and served as makeshift shelters whenever news of disappearances spread through the region. Savanna taught the others her techniques for scraping and hollowing out the earth and placing the fronds just right to avoid detection.

One night while on guard duty, Savanna dropped to the

ground and wiggled on her belly until she could peek through the heart-shaped leaves of a tangled yam vine. She watched the brazen slave traders skulk along a path carrying flickering lanterns to light the way. A twig snapped behind her and as she turned to investigate something clamped her mouth shut and pinned her arms together like a pair of tethered wings. A poacher, she thought, and realized that no amount of fighting or struggling would help her now. Better to save her strength and energy for the long journey ahead. She had never been on a ship and didn't know what it all meant. To her complete surprise, her captor relaxed his grip and whispered, "I'm here to help, not hurt you, and in turn, you can help me."

Unsure of the motives and identity of her new companion, Savanna turned and faced the stranger.

"I am here to help you survive and thrive as a protector and provider for your people. I have seen how you work and know how much you care. Your value as part of my growing community would be immeasurable. I'd like to share the gift of immortality with you so that you can carry on throughout time helping those you love."

Savanna gazed into crimson eyes which seemed to bob in the warm wind rustling the trees. She smirked, thinking her friends were playing a joke on her, but her heart raced and pounded in her ears as two fangs pierced the pulsing blue artery on her slender neck. A tingling sensation trickled through her veins and her toes unfurled as she fell to the ground. Something cool encircled her finger and she curled into a fetal position like a baby in a womb. The visitor picked her up and placed her in one of the new hiding places she had just dug and covered her with freshly cut palm fronds.

"You are now a guardian with special powers and privileges, a creature of the night. Feed on the blood of living things and practice hunting with the animals. They have much to teach. Eventually you will feast on humans but, until then, quench your thirst with our four-legged cousins. Live in the shadows, and by the light of the moon. There are others like you so be patient and survive."

21

CHAPTER SIX

I t wasn't the smell of buttered popcorn or the whir of cotton candy machines that lured Hobo out of the woods and onto the fairway of Dooley's 2015 Spring Fling Carnival. It was the tantalizing aroma of freshly killed meat that teased his taste buds and overpowered the stench of tiger urine and elephant dung that hung in the night air like rotting fish on a hot summer day.

He watched a burly man toss bloody chunks of meat toward pacing tigers and lions and glimpsed what might be a copper ring on the feeder's large hand. Garish neon lights blurred his vision and a gut-wrenching hunger made him tremble like a junkie needing a fix. The shrill screams of mortals riding a rumbling roller coaster ricocheted through his brain and icy pinpricks of pain stabbed his fingers and toes. He leaned on his polished walking stick and rested. He needed to eat.

Finally the worn-out carnies counted their money and beer-sodden customers stumbled to their vehicles for unsafe rides home. Lights dimmed and voices faded as the carnival broke down for the night. The big cats still smelled appealing so he crept quietly towards the holding area and laughed to himself when the lion tamer threw a limp human form into a cage. Another vampire! He was so blood sick he didn't notice the subtle essence of one of his own kind.

The starving vampire raised his walking stick in the air. "Good evening brother," Hobo called out to the surprised handler. "How's it going tonight?"

"Fine," the animal trainer answered after seeing the copper ring on Hobo's hand. "What's that you're carrying?" he asked pointing at the piece of wood.

"This is my favorite piece of organic equipment. I call it my Woodstock Walker. Doubles as a snack pack when I wrap some treats in a bandana at the tip and the little hole in the middle is an incense holder when I feel like burning some patchouli sticks. Great for fast food on the go if you know what I mean."

The trainer laughed. "Have you eaten yet? Plenty of leftovers." He motioned toward a small pile of bound humans with duct tape stretched across their mouths.

"I'm famished. Can we dispense with the formalities and chow down?"

They each grabbed a squirming human to feed on. Fear infused mortals were succulent and spicy. Their adrenaline soaked veins pulsed like swarming bees around a honey- filled hive and they tasted like a mixture of sea salt, crushed black peppercorns, and sweet agave nectar. Hobo savored the warm brew and drank until his body relaxed and his head stopped pounding. His new dining partner swilled his meal and tossed the remains into the large cage that housed the hungry circus cats. "I call that my personal garbage disposal system" he laughed. "They call me Bustah around here, as in I'll bust ya in the mouth if you give me any crap. Who are you?"

"I'm Hobo, nice to meet you. Got chased out of the last town I was in. Some paranoid idiot said I was stalking people. I wasn't stalking; I was shopping for a meal. Things got ugly and I left in a hurry. Ended up stuffing myself into a tree trunk and rested till now. Blood count was low and I started to get the shakes so when I smelled your little delicatessen here, figured I'd follow my nose. Nice setup. Ever get hassled?"

"Nope. By the time the local yokels are reported missing we're long gone. We have some stragglers from different parts of the country who follow us around and they end up as appetizers sometimes unless we really need some help. It's an easy gig. I travel, meet interesting people, and me and the kitties get a free all-you-can-eat pass everywhere we go."

Hobo laughed and patted his belly. "I better be moving on. I'm on my way to an important meeting. Thanks for the dinner and hospitality. Maybe someday I can return the favor."

Bustah nodded and waved as Hobo walked down the dirt road, content and satisfied like the purring caged cats.

CHAPTER SEVEN

Hobo walked a few yards, stopped, lowered his walking stick to the ground, and loosened a tattered blue kerchief tied to the tip. He unfurled a snow-white napkin, wiped his fangs, and shoved the stained cloth into the back pocket of his faded jeans. His penchant for carrying a stick over his shoulder like an aimless vagrant earned him the name Hobo amongst his immortal peers whom he would soon be seeing at the highly anticipated Vampire Preservation Society meeting. His scruffy appearance left no doubt that behind the grayish eyes peering out from rose-tinted granny glasses laid the soul of a hippie. His mortal name had been Jonathan Green and he had acquired his walking stick during his re-birth at age 20 at the infamous Woodstock Festival in Bethel, New York. The years leading up to his change affected society, too, on many levels.

During the 1950's individuality was frowned upon and cookie cutter homes in the suburbs and gas guzzling cars were considered status symbols. Smoldering beneath the tranquility and sameness of everyday life were the incendiary ingredients for explosive change when the swiveling hips and snarling lips of Elvis Presley catapulted the youth of the world into a whirlwind of cultural changes.

The next decade brought years of complicated

contradictions. The Vietnam War materialized on television sets in living rooms across the country and anti-war demonstrations became social battlefields for earnest protestors spreading messages of peace and love amongst the nation's youth. Jonathan embraced the multi-faceted hippie movement and focused on the budding green movement which dealt with environmental concerns as the push for progress became a major priority throughout the world. The movie *Easy Rider* roused his dormant bohemian soul and the new music blasting through transistor radios stoked his evolving spirit. The one constant in his life was watching his favorite television show *Dark Shadows* every afternoon and admiring the "vampire du jour", Barnabus Collins, who crept around Collinwood with a cape and cane baring his deadly incisors for all to see.

In 1969 the military draft weighed heavily on the minds of young men everywhere. Jonathan decided a weekend away from his pro-war parents was a good idea after he spotted a poster with a white dove perched on a guitar in a record store advertising *3 Days of Peace & Music* in White Lake, N.Y. He called his best friend Nik "Nickel" Stevens and they planned their weekend getaway.

On Friday morning, August 15, Jonathan shoved a few crumpled five and ten dollar bills into his back pockets and pulled a floppy suede hat tight over his head. Nickel wore a blue tie-dyed tee shirt, gray corduroy pants, and a red bandana wrapped around his forehead to keep his unruly brown hair in place. The two friends left the small town of Hanover, MA, hitched a ride straight to New York, and reached the musical mecca late in the afternoon.

Gray clouds scudded across the sky and people of all shapes and sizes converged in a large field filled with smoke, blankets, and whirling bodies. Jonathan smiled and turned to speak to Nickel but his friend was nowhere to be found. He pressed onward into the crowd looking for a small space to sit and wait. The smell of pot and incense floated in the air and chattering voices mingled with the whooshing sounds of helicopter blades transporting band members to the huge stage up front. A rumpled patchwork quilt looked abandoned so Jonathan placed his rolled up jacket on it to save a space for Nickel.

"Hey. Hey you," a female voice shouted from somewhere behind him.

Jonathan turned and looked around. A slender hand filled with silver rings poked a lit joint near his nose.

"Wanna hit?"

Curls of smoke snaked through his nostrils while he sucked on the glowing joint.

"Got anything to drink?" he yelled back to his mysterious benefactor.

"Sure," the voice giggled. A can of cold beer materialized as if by magic. "Keep it," the voice shouted, "and enjoy your trip!"

What trip he wondered as the chilled beer slid down his throat. Droplets of rain tickled his upturned face while he tipped the can back to empty it. He took another hit from someone else's joint and downed another beer.

"Let's dance," he yelled to no one in particular. Before long, swirls of neon colors filled his vision and the mass of people droned like bees and moved like an undulating snake. Jonathan lost track of time and himself; only the music and colors mattered to his drugged mind.

Suddenly everything disappeared. A forest of legs stomped squishy mud into his flushed face and several moments passed before Jonathan realized he was on the ground covered with cold mud and stale beer. His ankle throbbed and a stray foot kicked him in the forehead. Slowly he stood up and hobbled a short distance to a booth where a wrinkled old man sold trinkets and hand-carved walking sticks.

"Hey young fella, looks like you could use one of these," the wizened vendor rasped.

"Guess I tripped out there," Jonathan answered. "How did that girl know I was going to trip?"

The old man burst out laughing. "You and everyone else,"

he chortled. "You'll figure it out soon enough son. Here, take this stick and use it like a cane. I carved it myself. It's oak and will last a long, long time."

Jonathan reached into his pocket to fish for some money. The vendor waved him off. "My treat. Use it in good health."

"Thanks Pops," he mumbled, making his way to the edge of the crowd. He glanced around trying to find Nickel but only saw a mass of swaying bodies keeping time with the blaring music. Shifting his weight, Jonathan headed toward the line of port-a-potties hoping Nickel might be there.

"Hey Hopalong Cassidy! Over here, near the brown tent. I have something you can use."

The flap of the tent opened and the old merchant who had given him the walking stick sat cross-legged in the dark.

"Come on in. I have something to show you."

A gnarled hand grabbed Jonathan's sprained ankle and dragged him into the musty tent. Small pebbles ripped the tender skin of his belly and shards of pain shot through his foot. He clawed at the dirt trying to find something to latch onto but it was too late. The grizzled shopkeeper suckled the carotid artery of Jonathan Green's neck while Jimi Hendrix rearranged the "Star Spangled Banner" into a psychedelic symphony of sounds. It was the end of the festival and the beginning of a whole new life for the young man soon to be known as Hobo.

CHAPTER EIGHT

L
ucien LaPierre, affable host and owner of the huge castle, stood beside a blazing fireplace and scanned the crowd. His warm blue eyes danced beneath thick dark lashes and his chestnut hair fell on his shoulders like a wave of sap dripping from a black maple tree. Tall and well-built, with a face that caught the attention of many adoring women throughout the centuries, Lucien was easily recognized in the small community and admired for his expertise as an art historian. It wasn't long before he spotted Miranda, a former high school teacher in her other life, dressed in her re-birth suit of flowered bell-bottoms, white go-go boots, and a hot pink fringed top. She smiled and waved, fangs shining like lightning bolts against a dark summer sky. Artemis, a husky, bald blacksmith from Pennsylvania, clutched a bright red mug in his large hand and raised it in the air in a silent salute to the smiling host.

Lucien waved to several guests and nearly hit Hobo in the head. An odd mixture of patchouli and pot always clung to the hippie vampire like bad aftershave and cheap perfumed soap.

"Hi Lucien," Hobo gushed. "Can I get you anything to eat or drink?"

The older man smiled and shook his head. "No thanks. Go

mingle with the crowd. Introduce yourself to Miranda over there, the one in the white boots. She's from your era. I'm sure you have many things in common."

Hobo stroked his goatee and looked down at his torn jeans and scuffed boots. "Okay sir, but say the word and I'll get you whatever you need."

Not quite a stalker but irritating nonetheless, Lucien tried to be patient with the younger vamp's need for constant attention. Maybe one day he could find a project for Hobo to occupy his time and mind, something from the hippie era that would bring back fond memories of his mortal days. Lucien closed his eyes and smiled at the memory of his own re-birth in France during the mid 1600's.

Drawing and palettes of color always fascinated Lucien when he was growing up and crude sketches led to a serious pursuit of art. Intent on perfecting his own style, he let it be known throughout the countryside that he needed a model to sit several times a week for portrait painting. Late one evening, while studying the shadows of moonlight dusting the contours of his small room, he heard a tapping on his door and wondered who was out at such a late hour. He opened the door and stood face to face with the most beautiful woman he had ever seen in his life.

"May I help you?" he asked grabbing a candle up to get a closer look.

"I'm here to model, sir, if the position is still open."

He couldn't help but stare at her violet eyes peering out from a face as white and soft as gardenia petals blossoming on a warm spring day. Her lips were the color of crushed cherries and her hair a tumble of auburn curls. He reached out to touch her cheek but caught himself, not wanting to frighten her with such a bold move.

"Please my lady, come in. I did not mean to be so rude."

She stepped inside and smiled. "I really need the money sir, but I can only work after the sun has set. My father is quite ill and I must wait until he is bedded down before I can leave."

Entranced and smitten, Lucien readily agreed to the unusual stipulation without hesitation.

"I will see you tomorrow night then," he said guiding her to the door. "We can paint by the light of the full moon."

She vanished into the darkness like a banished apparition and Lucien soon realized that he had forgotten to ask her name. No matter, he thought. I will be seeing her for many nights to come.

The next day Lucien met with his fellow students to discuss and compare various shading techniques. He debated whether or not to tell his friends about his stroke of luck with the beautiful model feeling both protective and even a bit jealous at the thought of her posing for anyone else. He decided to stay quiet, not wanting to share her beauty in any other way except on canvas.

The afternoon sun twinkled between the willowy boughs of budding apple trees bursting with tiny pink blossoms. Lucien inhaled the sweet fragrance and basked in the warmth of springtime sun resting his head on a small bale of hay to think about the artistic vision he wanted to convey in his new project with the violet-eyed beauty of his dreams. He slumbered wrapped in the pastel hues of a setting sun.

He sensed her presence before opening his eyes and was surprised to see the full moon rising over the roof of his small home. He ran down a bramble-filled path and lit several tallow candles before she got to his door. He was waiting outside with a small lantern when she approached.

"Good evening my lady. Please forgive my ignorance. I neglected to ask your name last night."

"Angelique, sir, my name is Angelique."

"May I take your cloak Angelique?"

She lowered the velvet cowl from over her head and shook ringlets of shimmering hair free from her shoulders.

"I hope you like my dress," she murmured, handing him her cloak and smoothing the satin ruffles of her burgundy gown.

He nodded, so awed by her beauty that he couldn't speak.

"Shall I sit by the window where the moonbeams gather?"

"Yes," Lucien finally managed. "I need a few moments to arrange my palette. Would you care for some wine?"

"That would be nice."

Lucien turned, goblet in hand, and gazed into her bewitching eyes. "Please forgive me. Your beauty is beyond compare and I am most anxious to replicate your likeness on my canvas. Before we begin may I touch your face so that I may be further inspired by the sheer honor of working with one whose beauty surpasses all the angels in heaven?"

"Monsieur," she said softly, "I knew the moment I saw you that you would be hard to resist. You have awakened in me a yearning, a hunger shall we say, that has consumed my every waking moment."

She stepped closer and they held each other in a tender embrace.

"You smell of lavender, ma Cherie," Lucien whispered into her jeweled ear. "Lavender and..."

The coolness of her lips on his neck startled him. Lost in her scent and mesmerized by her loveliness, he ignored the stab of pain and flush of warmth trickling down into his chest and heart. Again and again Lucien smelled fragrant lavender as his beloved enchantress drank his blood until he collapsed. She tossed his limp body onto the cold hard ground and placed a small metal ring on his limp finger.

The rising sun blushed pale pink on the horizon when Lucien awoke, eyelids fluttering and burning as new optic cells multiplied. His nostrils twitched as he inhaled the sour smell of fear that still clung to his body mixed with the lingering scent of lavender. New incisors pressed against the soft tissue of his upper lip and a growing hunger rumbled through his tingling body. A small crumpled note tucked inside four copper rings rested near his head. He glanced at the flowery script. *"With this ring a secret lies, Hidden from all mortal eyes. Use it wisely as if to wed, And add another to those undead."*

CHAPTER NINE

A huge hand-carved grandfather clock struck twelve and roused Lucien from his reverie. He clapped his hands to gain everyone's attention. "Brothers and sisters of the dark, welcome once again to Nightshade Manor. Please join me in chanting our sacred oath."

Every voice in the room rose as one to chant:

"Immortal creatures, one and all

We share our love and heed our call

Protect each other and fill the need

The darkness always sets us free!"

Hobo tapped Lucien on the shoulder and distracted him once again. "Can I get you a drink or anything Mr. L?"

Lucien took a deep breath and tried to hide his irritation. "I'm about to meet with some friends. I suggest you do the same."

The hapless hippie followed Lucien as he walked to meet the others. "What are you doing?" Lucien snapped.

"You said I should meet some friends. That's what I'm doing."

"Not *my* friends, *your* friends. Now please, go back to the party and have a drink and enjoy yourself. I have business to attend to. If I need anything I'll let you know."

Hobo turned and walked towards a group of vamps

dressed in zoot suits and flapper dresses feeling smug about getting his idol's attention.

Jade, Wolf, and Savanna each sat on hand-carved chairs upholstered in lush black velvet in the meeting room as Lucien brought the meeting to order.

"Thanks for coming," he began. "I've just returned from our favorite resort, Club Dead, and as you all know, our regeneration package requires a sequestration in a safe, underground sanctum for a minimum of three months. I timed my return to coincide with tonight's party and I'm looking forward to hearing your reports so we can meet and greet the other guests out in the dining room."

Wolf looked at his companions, placed his leather pouch on the table, and Savanna put her sandalwood box next to it. Jade removed a folder from her briefcase and opened it on her lap. Clearly something had happened in his absence and Lucien felt the tension rise like bile in his throat after a bad feed.

Savanna picked up the sandalwood box and gently tapped the cover. "I've checked my census figures over and over hoping I made a mistake, but we've lost several members in our area and all we can find is blue powder and copper rings scattered around the country. I put them in here for safekeeping."

"My numbers are down, too, and I found the same thing." Wolf pointed to his beaded pouch lying next to the makeshift coffin Savanna chose to use.

Lucien looked at Jade.

"Here are my recent stats Lucien." She handed him the folder filled with printouts. "It isn't good."

Lucien thumbed through the paperwork and shook his head. "Nothing like this has happened since the days of hysteria in Eastern Europe hundreds of years ago. Certainly even witless mortals have advanced since then."

"Maybe it's some kind of vampiric plague like the one my people faced years ago," Wolf said.

"Is it possible that we're being stalked somehow? There's

so many new technological advances built into surveillance equipment we wouldn't even know," Jade offered.

Savanna shifted in her seat and looked at her friend. "I don't think so Jade. We don't have any body heat so they can't use thermal imaging and besides, what would be the point of hunting us down? We're the reason they've survived their Darwinian dystopia. They should be thanking us not killing us! Their arrogant mortal mentality prevents them from seeing anything beyond their own greed and malice. How many even know we exist? They're too busy planning ways to deceive and destroy each other with two-faced rhetoric and hidden agendas and can't be bothered with supernatural beings who have more intelligence and fangs-on knowledge than they'll ever have. Sorry but my dislike of mortals is one of the reasons why I enjoy sucking the life out of their decaying souls. It's part of my eternal psyche and I can't change that."

Music and laughter drifted through the halls and Lucien raised his hand. "Ok, let's not get ahead of ourselves. I understand everyone's concerns and we need to keep this quiet until we can come up with some answers. I'll hold the rings and ash here for safekeeping. We need to investigate further. Go out and mingle with our guests. Wolf and Jade, see if you can find two trustworthy assistants who would be willing to help with a reconnaissance mission. We need dependable people to scout out locations in the U.S. and report back to us from the road. We know so-called "regular" vampiric deaths result in disintegration of our bodies and repurposing of the rings so piles of blue ash and missing rebirth rings are certainly troubling."

CHAPTER TEN

Normally Wolf and Jade enjoyed working their way through the crowds. Jade's fans usually brought copies of her books for her to sign and Wolf's admirers often asked questions about Native American myths and legends. Tonight was different. There was a sense of urgency in their steps, an air of resolve and purpose as they glanced around the room. Sipping blood from crystal goblets and watching each other for signs of success in their search, both found their potential recruits at the same time.

Jade walked over to Skye Delane, a young Australian woman reborn while studying koalas and kangaroos in the wild. Her research skills and inquisitive mind were perfect for the blue ash mission and Jade knew she could be trusted. Plump and eternally tanned from her work outdoors, Skye enjoyed the serenity of large libraries filled with books and magazines and the hushed tones in museums and art galleries. She still wore gold-rimmed glasses and carried a notebook despite the fact that her vision was perfect and her memory enhanced by vampire genes. Jade was sure she'd be a willing team member.

Wolf followed his ears and heard Ren Davis, a former undercover cop with the Boston Police Department, sharing war stories about his patrols in Boston's notorious Combat

Zone. There was no mistaking the accent and attitude of an improper Bostonian and his dark curly hair and piercing blue eyes attracted many of the women who liked his bad boy persona. Big cities were his favorite and he fit in well with mortals who preferred the garish glow of streetlamps to the glare of sunny days. Wolf was certain he had found the perfect candidate for the job.

"Hey Ren, pahked any cahs lately?" Wolf shouted over the crowd.

Ren set his drink down and embraced his friend. "What's up my man? I was hoping to see you. What's happening?"

Wolf motioned towards the meeting room. "We need to talk in private for a few minutes."

CHAPTER ELEVEN

Skye and Ren waited in the hall while the four leaders talked amongst themselves in the meeting room. "Do you know why we're here?" Skye whispered, pushing stray blonde hairs away from her face.

"Haven't a clue," answered Ren leaning against the wall. "Good to see you though. Haven't seen you since the Women's Suffrage Movement back in the early 1900's. You ladies accomplished a lot back in the day."

Skye smiled at the memory. "Yes we did. I learned a lot about mortals, that's for sure. I remember the time you..."

Jade interrupted the conversation and motioned for them to enter the room. Long-stemmed glasses filled with fresh blood and frozen bloodsicles partially submerged in crushed ice lined a polished table nearby. Lucien welcomed them with a handshake and smile. "Please, help yourself to refreshments. We have a matter of great importance to discuss and I'd like you to feel at home."

Skye sat next to Jade on the couch. "We aren't in trouble, are we?" she asked, motioning towards Ren who stood by the blazing fireplace looking at the solemn group.

"No, not at all," Lucien said. "On the contrary, we need your assistance in ridding ourselves of some trouble."

Ren plopped his lanky frame into one of the cushioned

chairs. "Don't tell me it's those procreation punks again, the ones whose motto is 'He who sires the most is the best host'. Thought that problem was quashed when copper ring rationing went into effect as a kind of re-birth control program for vamps with repro-libido issues."

No one knew where the copper rings actually originated but they were part of vampire lore. It was believed that copper was chosen for use because it had germicidal qualities, was 100% recyclable, and was soft enough to size during rebirths. An unknown additive, perhaps a vampire version of DNA, was added during a secret smelting process and the rings shattered like fragile eggshells tossed to the ground once the wearer dissolved into grit. For those gifted with a shiny band, magical transformations into immortality became known as re-births and the lucky recipients were welcomed into the family. Over the centuries it became apparent that the copper bands needed to be tracked and guarded so they were scanned into a computer system, each ring bearing the essence of the wearer, and then were used as a census device to keep the tribe safe from extinction.

Wolf stood and walked over to the table where his pouch and Savanna's sandalwood box rested like a temporary cemetery for undead remains. "What we are about to reveal must remain in this room. Understood?"

Ren and Skye glanced at each other and nodded. This was serious and they both gave Wolf their undivided attention.

"Are either of you familiar with the history of The Vampire Preservation Society?" he began.

"I've heard some stories," Ren answered.

"Same here," Skye said.

"A brief history lesson before we go any further," Wolf said. "The leaders in this room represent the four races of man. We were re-born in various eras and in different parts of the globe and formed the VPS during the 1800's when the immortal community really started to grow. It was evident that some sort of tracking system was needed to protect existing members and to prevent overpopulation so we decided to use our copper rings as a census device. By observing mortals we learned that unrestricted population growth and pollution destroys valuable resources. We have been at the forefront of environmental activism and continue our conservation efforts in several ways, including screening potential re-birth recruits. We are now faced with an unusual problem and I'll let Lucien take over from here."

Wolf glanced around the room and smiled when Lucien began to speak.

"Our lives are at stake here, pardon the pun, and your discretion is crucial. It seems someone or something is destroying our members. We have re-birth rings and piles of blue ash in both the pouch and box on the table. We suspect mortals are at it again and need your eyes, ears, and noses to check things out and find the culprits. Needless to say, eliminate any killers you find."

Savanna stood, grabbed a pitcher full of blood, and refilled everyone's glass.

"Rather than take the time exploring the whole world," he continued, "we want you to spend a week monitoring cities and towns within the United States. Skye, you take the West Coast, and Ren, the East. Make note of any unusual mortal activities, choose a site for a rendezvous, and then report back to us by phone." Lucien reached into his briefcase and pulled out two cell phones handing one to each volunteer.

"These are burners. I have programmed our numbers and you can call each other, but remember, we don't need any mortal snooping agencies intercepting our calls or texts, so keep them to a minimum. Any questions?"

Ren and Skye stood, took a phone, and grabbed their glasses of blood. Ren raised his glass in the air. "I propose a toast to immortality and to all our fallen friends. Our bites really are worse than barks and payback is a cinch."

CHAPTER TWELVE

S kye loved the West Coast of America and felt like a chameleon perched on a leafy vine watching all the action from a hidden vantage point. She visited Ocean Beach in San Diego and walked the length of the OB pier at night listening to mortal conversations accented by crashing waves. She danced in nightclubs on Sunset Strip, rode a Ferris wheel in Santa Monica, and took a long bike ride along the boardwalk of Venice Beach. Each stop offered a variation on the same theme. She listened to the excited chatter of tourists and vendors, watched druggies and dealers do their stoned dope deal rituals, and ventured down dark, graffitied alleys always searching for a hint of hatred for her immortal kin. There was no sign of unrest and no unusual nocturnal murmurings from any of the vamp communes.

Time was running out and Skye headed to San Francisco where the Golden Gate Bridge beckoned travelers to head North and South over windswept water and roller coaster streets careened into pockets of people and places as diverse and multi-layered as the buildings they lived in.

Ren was coming to town the next night and Skye saved her notes and maps in the iPad mini she always carried for research projects and tapped the Done button. She knew the information would be safe. Encryption was mandatory for all communications and the algorithms and keys were changed frequently to avoid any problems. All devices were updated on a regular basis by professional programmers intent on ferreting out hackers and snoops. She sighed and placed the rectangular device back into the soft folds of her well-worn purse.

Skye was hungry and decided a stroll near Golden Gate Park would yield a taste or two. Aging hippies and wilted flower children often congregated in the park at night to smoke weed, play guitars, and trade stories of their peace and love days. It was hassle-free dining for vamps who wanted to hit and run and be done for the night. Skye chose a middle-aged man carrying a battered guitar slung over his shoulder. He welcomed the warm hug she offered and slumped in resignation once her fangs pierced his stubbled neck.

Thick coastal fog rolled in blanketing the city in tufts of patchy haze and Skye decided to call it a night. She stepped off the curb and heard a faint clink near her sandal, the sound of metal tapping asphalt in the hush of a semi-slumbering city. Curious, she glanced at the ground and noticed a dusting of bright blue powder on her painted toenails and a small shiny object twinkling in the bright shine of a glowing streetlamp. A few feet away two more rings sparkled in the dewy grass and beside them a small pile of blue ash jutted up from the damp soil like an ant mound waiting for a queen. She grabbed the rings and carefully scooped the ash into a small baggie scanning the area for any sneaky mortals who might be lurking nearby. Satisfied that no one had seen her, Skye returned to her cheap hotel room and put the Do Not Disturb sign on the outside doorknob. The room had no windows but taking no chances she crawled beneath the tattered box spring to get some rest. Tomorrow was going to be a big day.

THE VAMPIRE PRESERVATION SOCIETY

CHAPTER THIRTEEN

Ren enjoyed the nightclubs, underground cafes, and theatre districts of big cities invariably filled with strung out junkies, affluent yuppies, and homeless runaways clamoring to be part of a warped neon landscape called "the nightlife" by ignorant mortals. Ren's handsome looks and confident swagger complimented the mystique surrounding his persona and mortals were immediately drawn to his charismatic ways. He had no trouble feeding or gathering information in each city he visited.

The downside to this mission was the need to lurk in rat-infested, urine stained alleys watching the dregs of society puking and preying on the soused remnants of shuttered clubs and bars. As drunken patrons straggled home Ren listened and watched for signs of covert activity from any would-be vampire killers who might be lying in wait to murder one of his kin. He found rings and ash in Boston, New York, and Detroit but found no common denominators, no human footprints, and no mortal residue in any of the samples. He filled his small journal with coded notes and made his way towards San Francisco where he and Skye had agreed to meet. After grabbing a bite to eat in Albuquerque he found a small cave tucked inside the rugged red hillside of Chaco Canyon and rested for the night. The blue ash mystery was intriguing and his cop-trained mind contemplated each piece of evidence like a chess player in a national tournament. Nothing made sense and he was anxious to see Skye so they could compare notes.

The following night Ren waited patiently for Skye at a small table in the corner of Mickey's Blues Club, a popular watering hole near the Embarcadero in San Francisco. A skinny musician wearing a faded North Beach sweatshirt and paint-stained jeans coaxed mournful notes out of a well-worn Stratocaster that suited his gloomy state of mind. He knew Skye looked forward to returning to Australia and her research work and wondered how much longer their detective stakeouts were going to last.

He watched Skye enter the club via a side door and grinned as she sauntered over to the table. They both scanned the darkened room and made a mental note of other vampires in the club, sensing two in a corner near the restrooms, a minimal distraction from the business at hand.

A waitress appeared as soon as his companion took her seat.

"Would you like a drink?" he asked Skye.

"Sure. Bloody Mary please."

"Make that two," he said flashing a friendly smile.

The waitress left and Skye glanced around the club again. "Ren, I'm really scared! I've got a baggie full of ashes and some copper rings and have no clue how, why, or what happened. I didn't see or hear any mortal connections to this and got lucky finding the remains that I did. A few hours more and the rain would have washed the ashes away and the rings would have ended up in the sewer system. What then? How about you? Did you find anything?"

The waitress returned with their drinks and placed them on thin cardboard coasters shaped like acoustic guitars.

"Thanks," Ren said, winking and handing the attractive girl a fifty-dollar bill. "Keep the change."

Skye rolled her eyes and reached for her blue leather notebook. "Quite the lady killer, huh?" she giggled and they both laughed at the double meaning of her quip.

"What have you got?" she whispered across the table.

"Hold on a minute, Nancy Drew." He pulled out an engraved silver flask from the inside pocket of his black leather jacket and poured a few ounces of dark fluid into both drinks twirling a large celery stick around the rims to enhance the flavor.

"Home brew from one of the locals. Claims it's as good as Hemo-Sip with half the calories," he laughed sipping the crimson cocktail and watching Skye's reaction to her altered concoction.

New musicians took the stage and the tempo changed to a driving beat accentuated by the loud chattering of drunken mortals sounding like a swarm of pesky mosquitoes. Skye glanced at her watch. "Give me your notes," she snapped. "I'm going out back to call in our reports. It's too noisy in here and I'm getting a headache."

Ren patted his jacket pocket where he carried his journal and pointed to her drink.   "At least finish that."

She gulped the rest and rose from her chair. "Wait, I'll go with you," Ren said. "This drink is good but now I'm craving the real thing."

They made their way to the rear entrance and exited through a heavy green door into a narrow alleyway lit with garish orange light from a blinking neon sign nearby. Skye hit the buttons on her cell phone and after a moment heard Lucien's voice on the other end. Ren stood beside her and smiled when he heard their leader's voice.

"You're on speaker and everyone is here. We're all eager to hear what you've discovered."

"We're still in San Francisco and..."

A deafening howl echoed through the alleyway and over the phone. Skye screeched in horror as Ren disintegrated before her eyes. His death scream pierced the air as his immortal body exploded sprinkling cobalt blue ash on Skye's blond eyelashes and silken hair like luminescent glitter on New Year's Eve. She dropped her phone and heard a voice coming out of the speaker.

"What's wrong? What's wrong?" Lucien yelled.

"It's not mortals! It's not mortals!" Skye screamed over and over again. She shrieked one last time before dissolving into a powdery blue heap of ash, her ring colliding with Ren's beside the broken cell phone.

CHAPTER FOURTEEN

Jade sat cross-legged on the floor, eyes swollen and red from crying while Savanna rocked back and forth, knees to chest, in a futile effort to comfort herself. Hearing the death scream of kindred immortals was unpleasant and the high-pitched assault on ultra-sensitive ears lingered like an echo bouncing inside a cavernous well.

"What now Lucien?" Jade asked in a trembling voice.

The shaken leader poured fresh blood into a pitcher and refilled each crystal goblet. He stared at the silent phone for several minutes, trying to gather his thoughts.

"Must be the other group of misfits, the Re-Birth Regulators or whatever they call themselves nowadays," Wolf muttered.

"Renegades, they call themselves The Renegades," Lucien answered. "I'll arrange a meeting with their leader tomorrow evening. I find their lack of familial respect distasteful, but I have to put my personal feelings aside for our greater good. I'll go alone and report back to the three of you upon my return."

Wolf shifted in his chair. "Are you sure that's wise?"

Savanna stood and sighed heavily. "What's the problem? We're all brothers and sisters who are in this together. Renegade leader or not, he is just another vampire!"

Lucien looked up, a fang-filled grin flashing across his handsome face. "My dear Ms. Martin, what you're saying is true. However, there are a few details you and many others are unaware of. There are some angry, resentful undead who truly dislike those of us who enjoy our immortality, which is precisely why I must meet with their leader, no matter how unpleasant it may be. You see, my friends, the Renegade leader is an immortal sometimes called Rion by others in the outlaw communities, but his real name is Lucas LaPierre. He is my twin brother."

Savanna gasped and Jade stared, eyes wide and mouth open in surprise. Lucien stood, walked to a pile of wood, and threw a log into the smoldering fireplace.

"Let me share my tale of two strange siblings who once were friends completely devoted to each other as only identical twins can be. Wolf knows part of my secret but has never heard the whole story. Grab your drinks and get comfortable."

Jade and Savanna moved to an overstuffed, maroon sofa near the door and Wolf sat on the floor near the now glowing fire. Lucien began.

"My brother and I were close growing up. We were, after all, twins, and our bond was strengthened when our parents perished during the Great Plague. So many people died during the pandemic and it was heart-wrenching to see our parents suffer. I vowed to take care of my brother and protect him from harm. The demise of my family was excruciating and that memory still motivates me to protect and nurture all of our immortal members to this day.

After we buried our loved ones, we moved to another part of the countryside to try to escape the invisible menace, now known as the Black Death, which continued to engulf Europe and other countries. We worked together and became self-sufficient, learning how to plant gardens and feed ourselves with fresh fruits and vegetables picked right off the vine. Lucas enjoyed the feel of dirt between his fingers and the sight of tender sprigs of vegetables and fruits poking through fertile soil in search of sunshine and rain. I, on the other hand, saw the same fields awash in brilliant colors and muted tones embellished with textures and forms that only nature could create. I sketched, drew, and painted, trying to capture the essence of my artistic visions while Lucas plowed and planted his fields of dreams. We were orphans working hard with what little we had and we were content until that fateful night Angelique came along and turned me into a creature of the night."

He paused, letting his words sink in before continuing. "I didn't understand what had happened to me when I awoke that first night of being re-born. I pushed blood soaked leaves off my face and watched the full moon blazing across the tops of tall evergreen trees. Something shiny caught my eye and I found four copper rings near my head with a cryptic note tucked inside. Confused, I rose up on my elbows and touched my damp neck. An overpowering thirst twitched in my throat and, to my surprise, I heard the faint heartbeat of a field mouse in the tangled roots of a bush near my feet. I reached out and grabbed the furry body, certain it would bite and scratch its way free. I brought the soft creature close to my face and stared into its eyes, feeling its tiny gasps of breath on my face, its whiskers tickling the hairs inside my flaring nostrils. My mouth watered and I ran my parched tongue over newly grown fangs. The small head snapped easily, like brittle pussy willow branches on a cold December morning. I squeezed tiny droplets of blood into my mouth, savoring the taste and warmth, realizing that I would need to feed on blood from that night on."

Lucien took a sip from his drink and continued. "The beginning years of my immortality were difficult. I avoided my brother whenever possible, making excuses for my prolonged absences. At first I fed on small animals, roaming the countryside at night like a hungry shadow, but my thirst grew, and as you all know, the only way to quench bloodlust is to prey on humans so I did.

Eventually the desire for companionship overwhelmed me

and I longed for my sweet Angelique. I wanted to touch her silken skin and breathe in the lavender scent that captivated me each night we were together. I decided to use the copper rings she had left me and sired three friends rather quickly. Something went wrong, I assumed, when I couldn't find any of them after their re-births. They disappeared shortly after the change. I saved the last ring, hoping to find a female who would become my immortal mate in the event that Angelique had disappeared, too.

I traveled, sketched, and painted for many, many years, always hoping to find that one special being who was worthy of my gift. One night, after a delicious feed in London, I spotted the woman of my dreams dancing in the moonlight outside of a rowdy tavern. The sweet sounds of a violin drifted through the air and her blue satin gown swished with each delicate turn of her feet. Tousled curls bounced on bared shoulders and dangling earrings caught the glint of the moon shining overhead. She reminded me of my beautiful Angelique and the sight of her calmed the restless yearning that churned inside my body, mind and soul.

I walked up to her and gazed into eyes the color of a robins eggs hatched on a warm spring day. I grabbed her by the waist and we waltzed, feet barely touching the ground, swirling in circles and laughing with each step. Her face was as smooth as rose petals and she smelled like jasmine and mint and all that is fresh and clean in the world. I waited a few moments, fangs pressed sharply against my quivering lip until I could hold back no longer. I sniffed her sweet skin and opened my mouth, ready to savor the warm gush of blood. Her pale skin popped easily. I sucked for a moment and readied the last ring for my ultimate reward. My solitude was over; I had found my desired companion. I drank deeply and then, to my utter surprise, choked on some type of chalky goo that coated on my teeth and burned my throat. I opened my eyes and watched my new love disintegrate into a mound of grayish ash. Looking up I saw Lucas, wooden stake in hand and pure hatred blazing in bloodshot eyes.

'Lucas!' I screamed. 'What have you done?'

His hair, once as brown as the earth he loved, was now streaked with gray and silver. Small wrinkles accentuated his eyes and a thick mustache covered his upper lip. In a strange moment of recognition, I realized that despite the fact that we were twins, he had aged and I had not. I was staring at an older version of myself.

He smirked, pain and grief slashing across his face like a wild animal caught in a trap.

'What have I done?' Lucas shrieked. 'What have I done? Look what you've done all these years Lucien! I have followed you and watched as you killed and ravaged people. You have no morals. No decency. No conscience. I destroyed your abominable offspring as soon as they rose up from their stupor after you selfishly condemned them to the same fate you met. You are a monster Lucien, an evil, horrid thing and your reign of terror is about to end!'

Lucas trembled, raising a sharpened stake in the air, tears running down his weary face, disgust and loathing plainly visible on his face. It was more than I could bear. I grabbed the wooden weapon, tossed it into the dusty street, and pounced, slicing his jugular vein with my fangs, sobbing as I drank. His blood, once the same as mine so long ago, became my blood once again. The life-force of our parents now became the elixir of our dual immortality. I shoved the copper ring onto his limp finger, dragged his body to a grove of trees behind the tavern, and covered him with branches and leaves to shield him from the prying eyes of mortals and the light of a rising dawn.

'Rest in peace, my brother, rest in peace,' I whispered to his unconscious form.

It was several decades before I saw him again, and it was only for a moment in England sometime in the mid 1880's. He had become a renegade, a survivalist lurking on the fringes of our society, silently observing our growth and progress. He fashioned a copper hoop earring as a way to mock our re-birth rings and he still wears it today as far as I know. We haven't spoken in over a century and a half, but I do know where he lives. So there you have it, the tale of the twins. Now go! Feed! We have much to do!"

CHAPTER FIFTEEN

After the meeting, Jade and Savanna strolled around the castle grounds and made their way downtown until they reached a dimly lit coffeehouse called Witches Brew. Lilac-scented candles flickered on lavender checkered tablecloths and soft flute music drifted from speakers hidden in the oak rafters of the sloping ceiling. They sat at a corner table facing the street and ordered herbal tea from the barista at the counter. The atmosphere was soothing, a much needed break from the intensity at the castle.

"I'm glad we're not mortal," Savanna whispered across the table. "What short lives they have and they don't even realize it. They squander their time fighting with each other, destroying the environment, and fueling the greed that resides in their destructive souls. Wonder what it's like to watch your skin wrinkle and sag and how it feels to approach death with no knowledge of how to prepare for the failure of the soul and mind as it disintegrates into oblivion. How lucky we are not to have those concerns."

Jade sipped her chamomile tea, remaining silent for a few moments. "We may not have the same problems as mortals, but we certainly have concerns. I miss the warmth of sunshine on my face, the bright blossoms of spring reaching for the sky, picnics in the park, watching children run and play on freshly mown grass, and the sight of shimmering rainbows after gentle summertime showers. Right now I'm really concerned about the invisible threat we're facing. At least mortals have somewhat of an idea of what to expect in their life spans. We have no experience with this kind of problem."

Customers continued to trek in and out of the coffee shop with steaming paper cups or soft drinks in hand.

"Fast food," Savanna laughed as they watched the mortal parade. "Remember that English nobleman who fell madly in love with you Jade? What was his name?"

Jade's green eyes twinkled. "Sir Richard Miles. That was back when I was a baby vampire," she laughed. "Back when I first met Lucien."

"I'd like to hear that story," said a familiar voice from a booth against the wall.

Both women were so intent on watching the scurrying humans that they hadn't paid attention to any other activity around them. Wolf chuckled and slid across the aisle to join them at their table.

"Wolf!" Savanna playfully scolded. "You could at least make a bit of noise to announce your arrival. These damn mortals are so loud you can hear them without even trying. You're as quiet as a spider weaving a web."

Wolf pulled his chair closer and sipped from a covered thermal mug decorated with pentagrams, pumpkins, and hissing black cats. "They say you can bring your own cup in for refills, but they don't specify what the refills are. Care for some pig blood?"

"No thanks," they both answered. "We just fed awhile ago and took a break to window shop for our next meal. What're you up to?"

Wolf glanced around and lowered his voice to a whisper. "I needed a distraction from Ren and Skye's deaths. Their screams keep echoing over and over in my head. Lucien wanted some time alone to come up with a plan, so here I am. Now Jade, tell me about your admirer and how you first met Lucien."

Jade smiled and began her tale. "Back in the late 1800's, Savanna and I met in a miner's camp in Northern California after stalking the same territory for feeding grounds. As you remember, in those days whisky and rum were the drinks of choice for the grungy gold diggers so we teamed up to feed because it was easier to overtake the drunken morons who were so defensive and greedy, they carried guns, knives, and picks in backpacks to protect their prized golden nuggets. Little did they know their blood was the precious commodity, not their stupid rocks.

One night we decided to visit a saloon in San Francisco where I was re-born. I had mixed feelings about returning but Savanna convinced me that we could have some fun chasing the racist idiots. We wanted to see if city mortals were any different than the bums we were feasting on so I decided to wear a red silk gown and emerald earrings to match my eyes and Savanna chose pale yellow organza to highlight her soft mocha skin and cocoa eyes. We were stunning if I must say so myself."

Savanna giggled. "They all stunk as far as I was concerned. Nasty mortal musk in all its glory."

Wolf laughed and took another sip of his drink. "Go on."

"We entered a crowded saloon and I spotted a well-dressed man sitting at a large round table sipping expensive brandy and puffing on an imported cigar. He looked up as I entered and I smiled a dazzling grin that would haunt his nights and invade his days for decades to come.

For months I teased him, toying with him like a cat and mouse game of hide and seek. I hid in darkened doorways and littered alleys watching him search for me on nights when I didn't appear. When I did emerge after several weeks his face lit up like a lantern and his eyes sparkled with obvious desire. Part of me felt flattered to be an object of his attention, but another side of me felt pity for such a stupid creature who sat for hours hoping to catch a glimpse of his "fiery girl" as he called me. Finally, I just stopped going to that section of town at all. Savanna and I grew tired of dodging the locals and grew bored with the area, so we traveled together for quite some time, staying in places for a couple of years, sometimes only days, but always moving when life became too predictable and mundane. Eventually we parted ways.

Savanna went East to study the new skyscrapers being built in big cities and I continued to wander throughout various towns and cities watching the Iron Horse being constructed and helping the laborers when I could by giving them food and money I stole from abusive foremen. Some help was better than none. There wasn't much else I could do."

Wolf nodded in agreement. "My people hated the railroad and all the destruction it brought. We felt powerless to stop it. Sorry, didn't mean to interrupt."

Jade smiled and took a sip of her chamomile tea. "After nearly 20 years I decided to pay Richard a visit. I was curious to see how he had changed. Morbid curiosity I guess. Of course I looked the same and would be easy to recognize. I spotted him sitting at the same table where we had first met. His coal black hair had grown thin and white and barely covered the top of his pink scalp. His hands trembled when he raised a mug of ale to his chapped lips and dull watery eyes peered out from bifocals resting on his wrinkled skin. He had become a shell of a person, worn down by life and weary beyond his years.

I approached him, not sure of what to say or do. Maybe he wouldn't remember me, or perhaps I was the cause of his broken spirit. I pondered my next move, torn by a mix of emotions that contradicted the essence of who and what I had become. One side of me hated being immortal knowing I would never have children, never sit in the sun to warm chilled bones, or be married and cared for like a mortal women. The other part of me felt superior, more powerful and intelligent than anything else that had a finite lifespan. I was cocky, arrogant, and self-assured."

"Here comes the good part," Savanna interjected when Jade took another sip of tea.

"No, here comes the waitress." Wolf glanced toward the worn-out server shuffling over to their table. The coffee shop was empty.

"Sorry folks, time to go. We're closing up."

"No problem," Savanna answered. "We were just thinking of getting a bite to eat."

They all burst into giggles as they made their way out the door to stroll through town like wisps of vapor floating on damp cobblestone streets.

"I smell a meal," whispered Wolf as he headed down a darkened alley. "Let's break for a few minutes and meet back at the park."

They split up, determined to quell the knot of hunger twisting inside. Several minutes later, the three energized and refreshed creatures walked to a wooden bench near a dribbling fountain. Even the crickets stopped chirping, sensing the subtle vibration of immortal hunters.

"Okay, let's get back to your story Jade," said Wolf glowing with contentment. "If we get hungry again I'm sure there's a homeless vagrant tucked beneath a bush somewhere near here."

"I left off with finding my aged friend. I decided to confront him to see what his reaction would be. I took a single step towards him when my feet flew in the air and I felt an ice-cold grip around my neck. I clawed and twisted trying to escape, but each movement seemed to strengthen the viselike hold and made it worse. My throat tightened and I gasped for air as the room faded into blotches of gray darkness. I knew no mortal was capable of such strength, but I couldn't see who possessed such brute force. A strange voice growled in my ear as I slid to the floor.

'You are a fool, young one! Listen to me or forfeit your gift of immortality.'

Another vampire! And he was pissed! Slowly my senses returned and he pulled me up by the back of my neck and pulled me close.

'You are jeopardizing our race and endangering our

57

lifestyle. We have enough to worry about without you adding to the list with your stupidity! It is imperative that we survive. You, on the other hand, are dispensable. I will not hesitate to terminate your existence. You are one of many who have an eternal gift. What is given can also be taken away. Exposing yourself to a half-witted human makes a mockery of both races. Either use your talents wisely or I will use mine to do whatever is necessary for the preservation of our race. The choice is yours. You have ten seconds to decide or I will decide for you.'

Wolf smiled. "That's Lucien for you, perpetually protecting our species."

"Needless to say you made the right decision," Savanna snickered.

"I certainly did! I also learned never to cross Lucien again or any other leader for that matter."

"Maybe your next book should be "Bloodsucking for Dummies," chuckled Savanna.

"Ha ha," Jade said with a lopsided grin.

A faint light rose above the horizon and a bird chirped a greeting from a nearby treetop.

"Time to go," Savanna said, brushing off her jeans. "See you later."

Jade and Wolf hugged and they all went their separate ways to rest for the daylight hours.

CHAPTER SIXTEEN

Two nights later Savanna returned home exhausted and drained after working on a complicated architectural project. Her dislike of humans made her irritable when working with them for any extended period of time and the urge to grab them by their throats and tear into their carotid arteries became almost too much to bear. As a food source, she saw no need to consider their race as anything but a usable commodity.

The phone rang just as she laid her head on a soft silk pillow. I'll let the machine get it she thought wearily until Lucien's voice boomed through the room.

"Savanna, please call me when you get..."

She snatched the phone from the base and cradled it on her shoulder. "I just got home from finishing a project with a bunch of incompetent mortals. I swear, the only thing they're good for is fighting and biting! What's up?"

Lucien laughed. He, too, could only tolerate a certain amount of time with humans. He understood they were a lower life form, but it didn't make it any easier when he had to listen to them drone on about their problems and shortcomings, all of which were self-induced. Unfortunately, they all had to deal with the inferior race on a regular basis in order to survive.

"Don't worry Savanna. No mortals on this mission. As you

know from our talk the other night, my relationship with my twin has been strained over the decades. Our current situation is forcing me to resume communications with him. He abhors anything modern and I don't know how or if he stays in touch with the outside world. He isn't aware of our blue ash problem and I need to find out if he is losing members, too. Renegades are harder to track and less cooperative, but if we can establish a meaningful dialogue with Lucas, at least we'll have some idea of what is going on with the outlaw clans. Would you act as a liaison between us?"

Savanna grabbed a pen and piece of paper from the nightstand near her bed. "Give me directions on how to find him. I have some free time tomorrow night. How will I know him?"

"He looks just like me, only older. His hair is long and gray, streaked with silver, and most of the time, he pulls it back into a ponytail. He has a Fu Manchu mustache, a silver soul patch, ice cold blue eyes, and a copper earring and attitude that is hard to miss. He's pissed off at the world and at me in particular, so use your own judgment. If he's too antagonistic, leave. He's a bit eccentric so be forewarned. He's also very secretive about his personal life but I've heard rumors of some kind of business or job he might have. I'll be anxious to hear how it goes."

"Don't worry, I won't take any crap. Get some rest. I'll talk to you soon."

Savanna opened the doors on her cherry wood armoire and fluffed the pink silk covered pillows inside. It was more practical to sleep in the furniture rather than on it. Heavy wooden doors blocked any stray sunbeams and the inside locks insured privacy and safety. It was the perfect resting place for a rejuvenating slumber.

CHAPTER SEVENTEEN

The path to Lucas LaPierre's home was strewn with broken branches, huge pine cones, and scattered solar lights that zigzagged in no particular order. Each snap of wood or crunching pine cone alerted the hermit vampire to the approach of someone or something trespassing on his property. It didn't matter who or what the interloper was, in the end it would be mashed between saliva slickened fangs. A winding driveway led to a small home perched on a mound surrounded by small barbed wire bushes sculpted into bizarre botanical creatures designed to keep intruders at bay. The unwelcoming atmosphere reflected the owner's personality and most people took the hint.

Savanna drove slowly through a maze of obstacles, parked the car and gazed skyward as bats flitted back and forth from a roost high in an empty tree. Turbulent storm clouds rolling across the darkening sky added to the strange scene.

Perfect, she thought, looks like the set of an old Vincent Price movie minus the creepy music. She opened her car door and grabbed her brown leather messenger bag filled with spreadsheets, notes, and the sandalwood box. Not sure of what to expect, but prepared to leave at the first sign of hostility, she lifted the triangular brass knocker and tapped on the door. She waited a few moments.

No answer.

Leaves rustled behind her caught up in a gust of chilled air. She raised her hand to knock again and found her fingers gripped by a much larger fist attached to a tall figure towering behind her.

"Help you?" a deep voice whispered into her diamond studded ear. Sounds like Lucien she thought as the grip tightened. Her fangs twitched beneath crimson lips and a low growl purred in the back of her throat.

"I'm looking for Lucas LaPierre."

The pressure on her fingers loosened and a firm hand nudged her shoulder until she stared directly into the sky blue eyes of an older version of Lucien. "You found him. Who are you and what do you want?"

Although she knew the tale of the twins, it startled her to actually see Lucas in person. She felt an immediate attraction to the bad boy vampire with the shining eyes and familiar handsome face and smiled at him before answering.

"Your brother asked me to pay you a visit. My name is Savanna Martin and I'm one of four leaders who work with Lucien to improve vampiric relations both here and abroad to ensure the survival of our race. Is there somewhere we can go to talk like civilized demons or is your door stoop the best you have to offer?"

Lucas laughed and gently took her arm. "You may fancy yourself a leader, Ms. Martin, but for now you'll have to follow me. Despite what you may think, we renegades do have manners and are capable of being gracious hosts."

He opened the front door and with a sweeping gesture motioned her toward a sand colored sofa fashioned out of sturdy gray driftwood tied together with thick hemp rope. Savanna ran her fingers over the weathered wood and large knots admiring the organic feel and texture of handmade furniture. An oval shaped maple burl coffee table sat low to the floor in front of the sofa and the intricate pattern of light and dark swirls gave the room a rustic feel.

"Please be comfortable Ms. Martin. Kitchens are for mindless mortal chatter. I presume we have important matters to discuss otherwise you wouldn't be here."

Savanna sat and watched Lucas light several candles on a stone mantle above the unlit fireplace and took a moment to glance around the dimly lit room. Black heavy drapes covered each window and the rest of the house was sparsely furnished with the exception of a small freezer and refrigerator stacked in a corner of the tiny kitchen. Much like mortal conservationists and environmentalists, Lucas and other rebels lived uncomplicated lives she mused. Feeding was considered a necessity and nothing more. There was no excitement or enthusiasm attached to the act and many actually found it distasteful. She had heard stories of some who considered suicide by sunlight to be an appealing solution to their angst and several renegades bore scars on their bodies from aborted self-immolations. Lucas's voice interrupted her thoughts.

"First, let me welcome you to "Shadow House", a parody, of course, on my brother's grandiose Nightshade Manor. As you can see, my needs are few and my possessions scant. I noticed you admiring my furniture. I consider myself to be one of the first recyclers in an otherwise indifferent society. May I offer you some critter blood? Raccoon, possum, and, of course, the always popular pig blood."

Savanna grinned. "Critter blood, huh? I'll stick with pig blood. Thanks."

Lucas walked to the kitchen and returned with two mugs, handing one to Savanna before sitting on the floor near a carved tree stump table. They each sipped and smiled, staring at each other, mentally checking out aspects of each other's personalities.

"Ok, down to business," Savanna began. She handed him the small sandalwood box containing blue ash and copper rings. Lucas lifted the lid and peered inside.

"We're losing members to some unknown virus, bacteria, plague or whatever. Lucien wanted me to share this news with you and ask for your support and assistance. I know you two have bad blood between you, pardon the pun, but there are things you don't know about your brother or his work with the Vampire Preservation Society. He respects your solitary lifestyle but also wants you to be aware of the deadly threat we're all facing from some mysterious source."

Lucas's silver-flecked eyes sparkled over the rim of his blood-filled mug. He moved towards the fireplace and lit a small log resting on an iron grate. An intoxicating smell filled the room, an earthy aroma mixed with the subtle scent of animal blood. Savanna's nostrils twitched and she inhaled the enticing smells.

"My own concoction," Lucas murmured in response to Savanna's unspoken compliment. "A blend of imported soils infused with a variety of delectable constituents from the animal kingdom. I'm glad you like it."

The sound of his voice relaxed her. The longer they sat together, the more attracted to him she became. "Continue Ms. Martin. I'm anxious to learn more about my altruistic sibling."

Savanna opened her briefcase, removed a file, and read some statistics. Glancing up she noticed a frown settling across his face, a telling moment that revealed his concern. He shook his head in disbelief when she finished.

"We need your population data to add to ours, Lucas. This isn't about you and Lucien. It's about all of us. You need to put your differences aside and work together to find out what's going on. You can wallow in your disdain and hatred after this crisis has passed. Harboring a grudge against your brother harms us all in the long run. We need to band together before we become statistics on someone else's printout. If you take some time to get reacquainted, you might find you have more in common besides your shared bloodline."

A hint of anger flitted across his face as Lucas rose from the floor. Thunder rumbled outside followed by pelting raindrops hitting the windows like stiletto heels on a smooth tile floor.

"My kind of night," Lucas observed, eyes closed, fingers

drumming the foggy window pane.

Savanna wrestled with her surprising emotions, fighting her attraction to the outlaw immortal. She wondered if his lips tasted like coppery pig blood and whether his hair would feel like liquid silver flowing between her fingers. She coughed and reminded herself of the reason for the visit, then handed him a business card.

"Call me when you have a report," she said, reaching for the door.

"I'll call you even if I don't." He smirked, watching her walk down the path to her car.

CHAPTER EIGHTEEN

Lucas wasn't sure what to think. The blue ash intrigued him. He knew from his own experiences killing Lucien's spawn that dead vampires disintegrated into gritty gray dust and the rings disappeared, so this was truly a mystery worthy of attention. Tossing thoughts inside his head like cards in a casino poker game, he weighed the pros and cons of a reunion with his estranged twin. Obstinacy was one thing, but extinction due to ignorance was quite another. He owed it to himself and other rebels to be informed and make proper decisions in the event the threat mushroomed into an epidemic. He picked up the phone, dialed Savanna's number, and left a message on her machine saying he would be visiting Nightshade Manor the following night around 11 p.m. to discuss certain issues with his sibling.

He hung up the phone and glanced at the rising sun kissing the tops of nearby trees and readied himself for rest inside a hollowed out cypress log filled with rich fragrant soil. As he laid his head down in the soft moist darkness he thought about their last strange reunion in England over a century ago.

The streets and back alleys of 1888 London were smeared with blood and fear as Jack the Ripper slashed his way into the fabric of everyday life. Lucas was annoyed at the butcher's antics: the increased presence of Bobbies on horseback forced him to limit his hunting to certain areas of town where food was scarce and the lighting dim.

One night he was stalking a red-headed prostitute who was working in darkened alleyways near the center of town. He watched her push a disheveled john down onto a pile of dirty hay and saw him drift to sleep when she finished her job. She straightened her dress, slipped dingy white gloves on her stubby fingers, and hurried down an alley towards a pile of dilapidated wooden crates.

At the opposite end a drunken patron from a nearby tavern stumbled into the cobblestone alley and mumbled a monotonous song about lost love and broken dreams. A tall figure lurked behind the singing sot as he headed towards the pile of wood to relieve himself, but Lucas focused on the woman scurrying in front of him. He picked up his pace, anxious to feed and be done with the fox and hound game.

Once he quickened his step everyone rushed forward. The woman screamed and fell into a crate, the drunk ran to help her up, and Lucas came face to face with his brother Lucien. Both of them had bared their fangs in anticipation of a meal and were shocked to see each other between the cracked planks of wood. The frightened humans grabbed each other's hands and fled, pounding on doors and screaming for help. The immortal twins lingered for a moment staring into each other's eyes, then sprinted in opposite directions, clopping horses close behind.

CHAPTER NINETEEN

S alty ocean air whipped Lucas's hair into his eyes and slapped his cheeks as he walked down the path towards Nightshade Manor. He opened and closed his clenched fist, not sure of what to feel or how to react when he reached the heavy gate. Harker the Barker appeared from the depths of a darkened doorway and pointed at the sensor.

"You know the drill. Scan your ring and move along."

Confused at first, Lucas smirked and removed his copper earring. His brother always was one for protocols. Evidently that hadn't changed. "I don't have a ring, this will have to do." He ran the slender hoop through the scanner and smiled. "There you go. Have I passed the test?"

Harker chuckled and extended his hand. "Lucien told me you were coming. Said you looked just like him only a little older. You could have passed on that alone but rules are rules and I have a job to do. Welcome!"

Lucas shook his hand and smiled. "Thanks for the help. I'll be seeing you later, I suppose, once I leave?"

"You may not see me but I'll see you, sir. Have a good night."

Lucas closed his eyes and steeled himself for the unexpected reunion, reminding himself that it wasn't about their dysfunctional relationship but about their society as a whole and the ties that bound them all together as true blood brothers. He raised his hand to knock on the huge wooden door but it flew open and he stood face to face with a younger version of himself, grinning from ear to ear.

"Good to see you brother! You look well," Lucien said, pumping his twin's hand with both of his in a hearty handshake.

Lucas grinned. "So do you Lucien." Despite the resentment he felt towards his sibling, Lucas felt secretly pleased to see him.

A polished antique grandfather clock chimed eleven times as the two men ambled down the hall to a sitting room where a freshly lit fire crackled in the fireplace. Lucas glanced around the room and sat on an overstuffed chair near the blazing fire while Lucien walked to a small cabinet in the corner of the room.

"Care for a vintage spirit, brother? I saved some original bottles of Absinthe Ordinaire for centuries hoping we'd share some. Only the best for the LaPierre twins, I always said. Remember?"

Lucas laughed and nodded. "I remember. You used to steal the juiciest apples from the farm stands and hand them to me for the first bite. And then there were the fresh baked breads and rolls that you claimed fell out of baskets on the way to market. I have many good memories, brother, not all are bad."

Lucien grinned and motioned towards the cabinet. "Let's prepare this together, like the old days."

Lucas stood and helped his twin remove a bottle, two glasses, slotted spoons, and several small white squares of sugar and placed them on a silver tray in the middle of the table then watched Lucien pour the emerald green absinthe into two hourglass-shaped glasses. They sat side by side watching the tinted fluid trickle down to the bottom laughing like mischievous schoolboys.

"Ready for some magic?" Lucien asked between giggles.

Lucas slapped his brother on the back and looked into his eyes. "I've been ready! Let's visit with the green muse!"

He grabbed two sugar cubes and gently placed them on top of the slotted spoons. Lucien drizzled ice cold water onto the sugar and the bright green drink turned milky white.

"Here's to brotherhood, old and new," Lucien toasted as they clinked glasses.

"To the mysteries of surviving an eternal life," Lucas added wryly.

The twins sat quietly for a few moments, sipping the licorice flavored brew and staring into the blazing fireplace. Lucas shifted in his chair and studied the younger looking version of himself.

"Are we going to discuss our philosophical differences or is there a reason for this tête-à-tête?" Lucas asked. "Surely it isn't because you've missed me."

Lucien refilled their glasses and sat down.

"As Savanna mentioned, we have a serious problem. Someone or something is stalking and slaughtering our relatives. We lost two friends last week in San Francisco. We sent Skye Delane and Ren Davis out to investigate the possibility that humans were trying to be comic book vampire slayers ridding the world of demons, but, as it turned out, that was not the case."

Lucas leaned forward intent on hearing more. Immortality vexed him but he wasn't quite ready to give it up to some unknown force.

"If not mortals, then what?" he asked.

Lucien shrugged and placed his drink on the table. "Their last moments were excruciating. Their death screams still echo in my head when I think about it. Skye's last words were 'it's not humans, it's not humans!' and we have no idea what happened. We sent two experienced discrete vamps out to gather information and they were destroyed in an alleyway behind a coffee shop in California. I don't want to offend you, brother, but is it possible that anyone in your community might be seeking retribution for being re-born?"

Lucas rose from his chair and stretched. His black leather boots clacked on the gray granite floor as he paced back and forth before the fireplace. He rested his arm on the mantel and placed his drink next to a candle. "As much as I dislike the feeding process that is necessary for our survival, I am vampire enough to know that our society deserves to be at the top of the food chain. Being immortal is a curse, to be sure, but mortality and all its trappings is demeaning to the notion of life itself. We rebels don't agree with many things, but we aren't genocidal. I don't know what it is, but it's not the loner or outlaw crew."

Lucien gave his brother a heartfelt embrace and walked his brother to the outside door.

"Thanks for coming Lucas. I'll be in touch."

CHAPTER TWENTY

L ucas returned home and thought about the bittersweet reunion. It reminded him of the uncertainty he felt as a young mortal when the bodies of neighbors and friends struck down by the plague piled up along dusty roadsides rotting in the noonday sun. The same questions applied to this situation. What the hell was going on and how do we control whatever it is?

Shortly after his rebirth, Lucas realized that his parents' deaths were caused by the bite of a tiny flea carrying the Black Plague and he decided to explore nature more fully. During the late 1700's he nurtured his love of botany studying plants and herbs in the United States by secretly following famed botanist William Bartram whose works were well-known throughout several countries. Billy the Flower Hunter, as Bartram was called, was fascinated by the wild lands of the U.S. and his infectious enthusiasm for the flora and fauna of new lands made him a valuable source of information in Lucas's quest for knowledge. From the alligator-infested swamps of Florida to the rolling hills of Pennsylvania Bartram's journals detailed discoveries of everything from healing plants and restorative teas to warnings and drawings of poisonous snakes and other strange creatures.

Although it was difficult to work limited hours after sunset, Lucas kept notes of his own observations and read William's detailed writings while the members of the research expedition slept soundly nearby. He enjoyed the fact that immortality enhanced his ability to absorb and retain vast amounts of knowledge in a short time.

The night after his reunion with Lucien, he set out on foot to visit the loners who dwelled on the perimeters of local cities and towns. Nothing seemed suspicious and there was no chattering about strange incidents or events. While walking through a sparse forest near a slumbering city, he spotted several small mounds of blue ash and a few copper rings mingled within some underbrush beside a stone wall. He scooped the powdery remains into a small plastic bag and slipped the rings into the pocket of his brown leather jacket. He was even more determined to conduct his own research into the deaths but first he wanted to contact Savanna Martin. He punched her phone number into his cell phone and waited as the beeps and chirps connected him.

"Martin Designs, may I help you?" Savanna answered.

"Is this the Ms.Martin, girl wonder, designer by day, demon by night?"

"Who the hell is this?" she snarled.

Lucas laughed. "Relax Savanna. It's Lucas LaPierre. How are you?"

She sighed and then giggled. "Well if it isn't the happy hermit. You actually called and didn't use Morse Code or a carrier pigeon. What brings you into the 21st century?"

"Ah, Ms. Martin," he sighed theatrically. "Always observant yet never obtuse. I'd like to meet with you, at your convenience of course, to discuss a few matters of importance. I realize mucking around with mortals monopolizes a great deal of your time, but all work and no play can make vamp fangs decay."

Savanna groaned. "Hold on a minute Mr. Mouth. I don't see you attending any immortal soirees, so put your money where your fangs are and be sociable once every decade or so. How about Wednesday night?"

"Sounds good to me," he answered. "Oh, by the way, leave

your briefcase at home. This isn't a formal affair, not yet anyway." He grinned, pressed the disconnect button, and strode through the overgrown path to his darkened home.

CHAPTER TWENTY-ONE

On Wednesday night Lucas heard Savanna's prized Shelby GT rumble into his driveway and watched her walk along the path leading to the front door. He swung the door open, startling her, and she scraped her index finger against a barbed wire sculpture next to the doorbell. The scent of her blood hit his nostrils in an instant and his fangs pushed against the soft skin of his lips as he fought to urge to bite her. Lust and hunger sparkled in his eyes and he forced himself to look away from her to hide the desire and delight gushing through him.

"Good to see you again Savanna. By the way, nice ride," he said motioning toward her gleaming car. "Maybe someday we can get inside and push it to the limit, if you catch my drift." He winked and smiled. "Thanks for coming."

"My pleasure," she answered, stepping through the doorway. "I have to admit, you have my curiosity piqued. How did the meeting with your brother go?"

She walked to the driftwood sofa and sat down while Lucas went to the kitchen. "Better than I expected," he said over his shoulder. "Drink?"

"Sure," she answered picking up a copy of Architectural

75

Digest and a catalog of herbal products that lay on the burl table.

"Pig blood, if I remember correctly."

"Good memory, for an old guy." She smiled. "Been reading?"

Lucas handed her a mug and glanced at the glossy magazine. "I try to stay informed about many things, including the work of my brother and his associates. He is not, however, familiar with my work or interests. I've chosen to keep my life secret from him."

Savanna settled back ready to listen. "What do you do?" she asked. "I was told you didn't care for modern gadgets and that you basically work on survival techniques spending most of your time alone."

Lucas placed his mug on the table and sat next to Savanna, looking into her eyes for a moment before speaking. "Let me ask you a question before I answer. What exactly do you know about my sibling and me? Did he give you any details of our unusual relationship or just the Reader's Digest version?"

She shifted uncomfortably, not sure where the conversation was going. Choosing her words carefully she answered. "I know what I need to know. Contrary to what you may believe, your brother has a great deal of respect for you. He mentioned your love of gardening and how you enjoyed working with the earth. That's more than enough information for me, but if you care to share any additional facts, go for it."

Lucas sat back and felt a sense of relief trickle through his shoulders. "I won't bore you with too many details, but I'll give you a brief overview of what I've been doing for the last several decades. As you know, with all the advances throughout the modern world, in some ways we've lost touch with our natural roots. I've always been fond of horticultural studies and trying to find new ways of growing and developing plant-based products and foods. After my re-birth I hated everything. Trees, plants, fruits, seeds all meant nothing to me. I felt as shriveled and bitter as rotted apples

76

decaying beneath dead trees.

One night while hunting I was chased into a field by an angry horseman whose daughter was going to be my next meal. I ran into a barn, tossed a lit lantern onto a bale of hay, and scrambled through a hole in the back of the building running and stumbling until I fell into a fragrant batch of snow-white jasmine. I laid there for a moment, eyes closed, nose twitching, and listened to crickets chirping a sweet serenade while the scent of tiny blossoms washed over me like a cool, crisp shower. I crushed several fragile flowers between my fingers and inhaled, surprised that something so small could smell so wonderful. I grabbed a clump of moist soil and rubbed it beneath my nose, the same smell of a budding field when the first drops of rain release the earthy aroma of soil. I remembered it all and rekindled my passion by making a pact with myself to channel my energies toward certain goals and to never let myself become a caricature of a monster again."

Savanna listened intently and sipped from her mug as he continued.

"I went on to pursue my studies and eventually started a business called L.L. Greens. I sell high quality herbs and supplements and am currently developing new lines of self-sustaining, eco-friendly products that will enhance the environment and not destroy it like mortals always manage to do. So, my dear Ms. Martin, that's the gist of it. I hope I didn't put you to sleep."

Savanna looked into his eyes and smiled. "We all have stories, Lucas, some good, some bad," she said shifting her position on the sofa. "I must say, yours is a bit unusual in that you seem to be in a profession that helps mortals survive and stay healthy. Isn't that a contradiction?"

Lucas threw his head back and laughed a deep resounding sound that echoed throughout the candlelight room. "Don't you see Ms. Martin, the delicious irony of it all? By helping the few mortals who are aware enough to realize that natural products are actually better for them, I am, in reality, helping our people by improving the quality of *our* meals and turning humans into *our* nutritional supplements. It's just a different way to utilize organic techniques for food production. Don't you agree?"

They both laughed and Savanna admired him even more. Somewhere in the small house a clock struck midnight.

"I have to get going Lucas. We're still working on the special project but there's nothing to report yet. We're losing vampires every day and trying to keep up with the sectors is exhausting. Your brother is on top of things. I give him credit for that and you should too."

She stood and stretched. Lucas sauntered over to a small table, opened a drawer, and then walked toward her until they stood face to face. He reached out and touched her cheek, eyes gleaming like sparklers on the fourth of July. He ran his finger over her quivering lip and pulled her to him, lips grazing each other, ending in a passionate kiss. He ran his tongue over her fangs feeling the cool smoothness of the sharpened teeth, enjoying the intimacy of touch. They embraced for a moment, then like two teenagers caught by their parents, jumped apart and smoothed their clothing. Savanna grabbed her purse and headed for the door.

"By the way," Lucas said handing her the copper rings he had found. "These are from my outposts. Please tell Lucien that I have cautioned my people to be alert and aware of any suspicious activities. They'll contact me if anything out of the ordinary happens."

She nodded and walked out the door. Both of them weren't sure what to make of their moment of passion but were pleased that it happened.

CHAPTER TWENTY-TWO

The following evening all four leaders met at Nightshade Manor to discuss the increasing reports of copper rings and blue ash being discovered around the country by frightened and confused members of the vampire community. A unanimous decision was made to release a limited amount of encrypted information to certain members including an advisory to report any suspicious activities, both mortal and otherwise, to sector leaders. Those chosen to receive the messages were responsible for passing the information along to others so that no electronic footprints could be traced back to their leaders.

Anxious vampires gathered in basements, homes, coffee shops and anywhere else where Wi-Fi signals could be captured by electronic devices to decipher hidden messages on laptops, tablets, and smart phones. A communal hush fell throughout all the gatherings as Lucien's words flashed across screens in secret coded script.

"Sisters and brothers of the night! We are acutely aware that we have lost some members and so far, we have no explanation. We are working around the clock to find a solution so until the problem is resolved, we must refrain from initiating any new re-births. We cannot afford to have an increase in population while an unknown enemy wreaks havoc within our existing clans. Periodic updates will be given as warranted. Until then, please hunt with extreme caution and report any sightings of blue ash remnants and or copper rings to your sector leaders. Be aware and feed with care."

After several minutes all screens flashed to black and the message was deleted by a specialized software program originally used by the mortal government for their clandestine operations. Jade swiped her finger across the top of her iPad and shut it down.

Wolf looked up from his notebook and started to speak. "Do any of you think it's possible that some kind of mutated virus is invading our immune systems, like mortal diseases that attack human bodies?"

Savanna looked up and nodded. "Good theory Wolf, but how could we test that hypothesis?"

Wolf scribbled a diagram as he spoke. "We need to find and observe someone in the beginning stages of this curse, maybe collect a blood specimen from one of our own and examine it under a microscope. We could gather some volunteers who might not be feeling well and get an assistant to examine them and take notes."

Jade chimed in. "I understand what you're saying, a baseline study group to see if we can track any symptoms or signs of trouble to catch it before it spreads. I think that's a great idea."

Lucien stood and walked over to the unlit fireplace. Savanna watched him closely to see if she could read his mood. He seemed pleased that his brother had turned over the ashes and rings he had collected but appeared to be concerned about their fragile alliance.

"We need to be very discreet with all this," he began. "I want to keep Lucas informed about what we are doing but I think we need to use some kind of a story to attract volunteers without causing a panic. Perhaps we can borrow a strategy from mortals and lie about an experiment we're conducting to test a new drink derived from manufactured platelets. The hook will be that anyone feeling sluggish or rundown is eligible to apply for a chance to enhance their metabolism and increase their hunting skills. We'll call it the "Blood Blast Project" and participation is free."

Word spread quickly and the following Friday night ten volunteers formed a line in the basement of the stone castle. They stood milling around and sharing stories of their favorite hunts and prey. They had all recently fed on mortals but weren't feeling as energized as usual. Edgar, a stocky vampire clad in tee shirt and jeans, moaned and sank to the granite floor, face tinged blue, pink spittle dribbling down his chin.

"My eyes, my eyes!" he shrieked, clawing at his face with flaky, swollen hands.

Screams echoed down the hall as Edgar disintegrated into a heap of blue ash. His copper ring rolled across the floor coming to rest at the feet of another volunteer. The remaining recruits scattered, clasping their ears and shaking their heads. A young vampire ran up the stairs two at a time and yelled help with every step he took and another vampire clad in tan scrub pants and shirt scooped up some ash and grabbed the errant copper ring.

Lucien and Wolf heard the commotion and rushed downstairs into the small make-shift office of volunteer lab assistant Matt Palmer, a pre-med student whose re-birth coincided with the turn of the century in the year 2000. Matt's work area had once been a dungeon back when the castle was used for other means and the faint aroma of blood and fear lingered within the old masonry walls. Matt looked up as Lucien and Wolf hurried through the door.

"I managed to salvage a few cells from the newly departed Edgar Munroe. Based on the other samples you gave me, it appears the gestation period of the virus or a bacterium is quite short and varies from individual to individual. Edgar fed a few hours ago and seemed fine, other than a few minor complaints that didn't seem important at the time."

Motioning towards the vials of blue ash lining the table behind him, he peered through a microscope while talking.

"Each sample is crawling with an amoeba-like form that splits into irregular shards and then migrates towards other pieces until it becomes whole again. There is a subtle change in the overall appearance once the form resolidifies. I think there is a slight mutation when the cells are separated and once they are joined together again, some sort of catalyst generates a destructive symbiosis between the newly formed organism and its host. I need more information on the hematology of diseased mortals before I can proceed. Any chance of acquiring some blood samples from sick mortals? I know it's a stretch but I really think it would help us get to the bottom of this problem."

Lucien looked at Wolf and replied. "We'll get on it right away. Thanks for your help Matt. We'll be in touch."

Lucien led Wolf through a maze of corridors and small rooms hidden deep within the bowels of the manor until they finally exited through a heavy iron door that opened onto a narrow cobblestone walkway snaking through windblown bushes and bare bent trees. The Atlantic Ocean churned below a jagged cliff, smashing white-crested waves on the rugged beach rocks as if to beat them into submission. Wolf half closed his amber eyes and braced himself against the strong, salt-flavored winds whipping his long black braid and burning his bronze-colored cheeks.

Lucien stared out over the deep dark water and watched four seagulls glide on invisible thermal currents. A huge rat poked its nose through a nearby bayberry bush and then scuttled across Lucien's brown leather boots in search of a morsel of food. Before its skinny pink tail could touch the ground Lucien snatched the wandering rodent, snapped its neck and caught a few droplets of blood on his tongue before handing the warm carcass to Wolf who squeezed a few drops of blood from the limp creature and then tossed it into the swirling ocean waters below.

Both distraught vampires threw their heads back and howled like wolves baying at the moon. To mortals it was the sound of wildlife owning the night and marking nocturnal territories. Immortals knew it as vampiric keening, an expression of mourning and loss seldom expressed in their coveted world.

"Well brother, sorry it comes to this," Lucien said. "We need to move fast before we lose more family members. Let's go to the city, infiltrate a mortal medical facility, and steal some decaying blood. Up for a non-caloric, non-nutritious, inedible blood hunt?"

Wolf smiled and patted Lucien's shoulder. "Bloody right I am," he answered in a perfect British accent. "Let's go find some dead red corpuscles!"

CHAPTER TWENTY-THREE

A neon exit sign glowed over the back door of Down Town Labs, a small non-descript facility nestled between a family-owned bakery and a newly painted gift shop selling lobster oven mitts and other the local kitsch. Wolf watched Lucien deftly twist the lab doorknob and push his way into the darkened office. He followed, glancing at the dim fluorescent light flickering over a stainless steel sink and smiling at the *Give Blood* posters lining the pale green walls. The smell of stale coffee wafted through the air, but the strong smell of newly drawn blood invigorated him.

"Be sure to check labels," Lucien whispered gesturing toward the stainless steel refrigerator. "If it's over a week old don't take it."

Wolf opened the door and quickly unscrewed the refrigerator light bulb. Using a flashlight he scanned the dates. "Lucien, these containers have different colored tops. Some are red, some yellow, some lavender and others are swirled colors. How do I know which is what?"

"Take one of each and we'll sort them out later."

Wolf grabbed the slender vials filled with crimson fluid and placed them in a small yellow cooler. His mouth watered and his stomach quivered as his blood thirst grew but he controlled the urge to pop the top off one of the small containers for a taste of refrigerated brew.

"Hurry up," Lucien said urgently, heading for the door. "I'm hungry and want to get this over with."

Wolf nodded and closed the cooler lid. He grabbed the handle of the blood-filled container and noticed a splash of light beaming through the front window of the building near the lab waiting room.

"Night watchman," Lucien murmured walking towards the back of the office. "Check out time." Both vampires disappeared into the sleepy streets of the city.

After a quick feed beneath a weeping willow tree they hurried back to Nightshade Manor and delivered the cooler to Matt's brightly lit office. Neon pink and orange markers were scattered on the floor beside textbooks, magazines, and printouts of medical literature. Matt sat on the floor next to the pile, tea colored hair spiked on top of his head like a rooster comb and black frame glasses perched on his thin nose. He closed his laptop and stood to greet the two anxious looking leaders.

"Do you think these samples will help?" Lucien lifted the blood-filled vials out of the small container. "We checked the dates and these specimens are fresh, but we don't know what the different colored caps mean."

Matt peered at the neatly arranged flacons and leaned against the jumble of pallets he had collected to fashion a temporary shelf for testing his theories. He sighed and looked at Lucien and Wolf.

"There is considerable danger trying to analyze infected samples, especially since we don't know what we're dealing with," Matt said. "A single drop could contaminate us or multiply on contact or... I don't have any sophisticated equipment but I do know that each colored cap has some significance as far as testing is concerned. I may have flunked out of medical school but I still remember some things. I'll use my microscope and whatever else I can lay my hands on to do some rudimentary comparisons between human samples and ours and see what happens."

Lucien glanced at Wolf then tapped the blood filled cooler with his index finger. "Do the best you can, son. That's all we ask."

CHAPTER TWENTY-FOUR

Matt pulled on a pair of purple latex gloves and carefully opened each vial one by one. The microscope and textbooks helped guide him as he compared the tainted human fluid with the blue ash of his newly fallen brethren. Before long a sliver of sunlight poked through a tiny crack in the vaulted ceiling high above his head signaling quitting time. He laid his head down on a piece of dusty burlap and slept the dreamless slumber of an exhausted immortal.

Upon rising the next evening Matt jogged into town for a quick feed and found a vagrant dozing on a rusted park bench. His fangs pierced the pulsing carotid artery easily and when he was finished he grabbed a rumpled newspaper to wipe his mouth after the meal. He spread the paper out and scanned the bold print headline. Clutching the blood-smeared newsprint in his hand, he raced back to his office muttering to himself as he reached for a textbook and glass slide. Several minutes passed while he jotted notes and numbers on lined sheets of paper and grinned as he drew arrows and lines linking thoughts to paper. An hour later he reached for his cell phone and called Lucien.

"Sir, sir, I think I've found the problem. Can you come

down to my office as soon as possible?"

"On my way," Lucien answered. Matt hung up and was startled to see the older vampire peering at him intently. Matt held up the newspaper and Lucien read the print.

AIDS EPIDEMIC CLAIMS MORE VICTIMS

Lucien shook his head and grabbed the paper out of Matt's hands. "Are you suggesting we've contracted a mortal disease? Is it even possible?"

"Yes," Matt cried out. "Tainted blood! Our people are feeding on diseased HIV infected mortals! The virus somehow mutates and invades our immortal immune systems. We're killing ourselves by feeding on the very substance that keeps us alive and blue ash is the remnants of our infected cells."

He sat heavily in his chair and looked up at the distraught leader. "Viruses mutate all the time and this one has somehow crossed over our blood brain barrier. Problem is, we've never encountered anything like this before. I hate to admit it, but we may need to recruit a human doctor who is familiar with this issue and bring him in for a consultation. We simply can't do it ourselves. Its unchartered territory!"

Lucien frowned and a ripple of concern flashed in his eyes. "Please keep that thought to yourself until I tell you otherwise. That would be a last resort. We have another meeting scheduled for tomorrow night and I need to consider our options. Please consider some other alternatives. I'll be back in a few hours."

Matt grabbed a notebook and sat down on the floor in front of his laptop. Lucien was gone before his butt hit the oversized cushion that doubled as a chair.

Lucien roamed the quiet streets of Gloucester listening to weary fishermen telling tales of the ones that got away. He enjoyed their banter and admired the hard work of fishing fleets battling the harsh ocean in order to feed their families. He never fed too close to home and at times like these when his emotions collided with the needs of his vampire community, he preferred to snack rather than have a full meal. It kept his senses sharp and his mind focused on the problem at hand.

An hour before dawn he returned to Matt's office and watched the studious young vampire work with the stolen vials of blood.

"Anything to report?"

"No progress at all, I'm afraid," Matt answered glancing up from a pile of papers on his desk.

Lucien sighed. "I appreciate your efforts," he said quietly. "I intend to broach the subject of mortal intervention at the meeting. Of course no one will be pleased, but I can't think of any other way. If we are fortunate enough to find a human assistant, I suspect negotiations will be difficult if not impossible. In the meantime I'll send Hobo to help you gather all the blue ash. We'll lock it in the vault upstairs and he can be in charge of safeguarding the copper rings. Last thing we need is for someone to get a hold of our remains. Now, go feed. You're as pale as the moon."

CHAPTER TWENTY-FIVE

At midnight the next night, Wolf, Jade, and Savanna waited for Lucien to be seated inside the candlelit meeting room at Nightshade Manor. "Tonight's meeting will be short," Lucien said as he strode into the room. "I know you're all hungry and need to feed soon so I won't keep you any longer than necessary."

Jade and Savanna glanced at each other and smiled. They had discovered an abundant feeding ground swarming with meandering mortals but the real problem was trying to determine which humans were safe to dine on. Wolf looked up from his leather-bound journal and met Lucien's gaze.

"There are ten more members lost since last night," Lucien began. "Our families need to be more cautious and less complacent about the issues we are facing."

Savanna nodded and chimed in. "We need to find a way to spot polluted food sources and pass the information along. It's hard not knowing what we're facing as far as contaminated meals are concerned. Is this going to create a food shortage? Do we need to think about stockpiling frozen platelets? I mean, we need to come up with some answers pretty soon or we'll be extinct and no one will even know!"

Somewhere in the distance a church bell chimed and broke

the silence in the tension-filled room. Sadness settled in Lucien's chest and his shoulders drooped as he prepared to deliver the lab assistant's findings. "I spoke with Matt last night. He's our volunteer med school dropout who's working on our problem and he has been able to isolate parts of a mutated virus. Evidently there are some common traits between our remains and those of certain diseased mortals. I am loathe to report that our friends and fellow immortals have contracted the human equivalent of the AIDS virus and there is nothing we can do about it at this time."

Jade gasped and Wolf jumped out of his chair while Savanna sat too stunned to speak. "Let me get this straight," Wolf said incredulously. "Mortal scum who have already destroyed my people, the environment, and each other are now causing the decline of our population? How can this be?"

"It's the virus my friends," Lucien answered slowly. "It adapts and mutates in our blood and we become host to the parasitic entity it becomes, similar to the Black Plague that killed my loved ones before I was re-born. I'm as outraged and sickened as you, but we need to think clearly and act responsibly. Matt has suggested an alliance with a mortal doctor versed in the treatments of AIDS in mortals who may be able to devise some safeguards for us so we don't starve to death. We will only last so long as a species with manufactured blood and supplements. I realize it's risky and there are strong anti-mortal sentiments among members in this group, but we have no alternative. Blue ash is turning up everywhere and we need to take whatever steps are necessary for our survival."

Savanna's eyes widened and she licked her glossy lips before speaking. "Are you suggesting we actually collaborate with one of our foes? It has never been done! We can't risk the exposure. Absolutely not! They can't be trusted. They're an inferior race and lack intelligence. I mean think about it. They actually lay outside in the sunlight, toasting and burning their skin like the meals they cook in their own ovens and grills. How smart is that?"

Despite the seriousness of the conversation, everyone chuckled as visions of roasted humans danced through their heads. "Rare, medium, or well-done," Lucien laughed as he remembered the meals he had eaten at beach resorts and coastal towns across Europe and the Mediterranean; cracked skin exposed to too much sunlight tasted like old leather wallets and others smelled of coconut and gardenia lotions and oils. He took his time with those, savoring the gentle nibble of soft cinnamon colored skin slightly taut over pulsing veins and delicate snow-white skin was the easiest to pierce, barely touched by sun, wind, or rain it was almost translucent.

Savanna clapped her hands and broke into Lucien's reverie. "So please continue. My insides are growling from hunger pangs."

"We need to take drastic measures," he continued. "I realize that cavorting with mortals for reasons other than sustenance is distasteful but we really have no choice. Let's adjourn for now and meet again in two nights for a strategy session. All this talk of mortals has me famished and I'm sure you feel the same."

Savanna snatched her purse from the table and stomped out the door. Jade trailed behind her, lost in thought and visibly upset. Wolf closed his journal and tucked it in the waistband of his jeans. The proposal was alarming to all of them. The ramifications were staggering and the logistics overwhelming. This was going to be a difficult task.

CHAPTER TWENTY-SIX

O nce again the four leaders gathered outside on a small patio facing the Atlantic. A blustery ocean breeze sprayed a mist of salty water onto the flat granite walkway and coated the wrought iron furniture with a damp sheen. Jade shivered and wrapped her light blue Pashmina shawl around her slender shoulders. "I have some ideas to share," she said as pounding waves crashed behind her. "But the ocean noise is too distracting and reminds me of the difficult times I had in San Francisco. Let's go inside so I can hear myself think."

They reconvened at a polished mahogany table in the dining room. Candles glowed in wooden sconces along the walls and in a crystal candelabrum hanging from a large wooden beam. Lucien served warm blood from a golden carafe. Jade nearly spilled hers when she plopped her latest book, *Sister Solutions,* on the table in front of Savanna.

Jade Lee's best-selling novels, called "Lee's Reads" by her horde of faithful fans, were fictionalized tales of two sisters, one a detective, the other a forensic specialist, who worked on murder cases together. Unbeknownst to the humans, the books served as a primer for roaming vampires giving tips on how to dispose of bodies and suggestions on how to avoid detection in a growing high tech world. Both humans and vampires enjoyed her crime solving stories and her second and third novels catapulted to number one best sellers within days of their release.

"I think I know how we can approach a mortal doctor. I've thought this through and feel confident that I can screen candidates to find a suitable mentor, doctor, advisor – whatever you want to call him or her."

"Are you willing to risk exposure and/or death if this scheme fails?" Wolf asked.

"I'm concerned too," Savanna added thumbing through *Sister Solutions*.

Lucien remained silent, crossing his long legs and settling back into his chair to listen.

Jade pointed to her book and grinned. "That, my friends, is my admission ticket to wherever I want to go! Like it or not, I'm a public figure and I can use that to my advantage to get access to people and places that might otherwise be off-limits. There's an AIDS symposium in Boston next week led by a Dr. Marcus Blackwell who has compiled a great deal of data on the disease by studying patients across the world. He's currently seeking funding for continued research and is, by all accounts, a compassionate doctor who cares for his patients as people rather than statistics scrawled on scraps of paper."

"I still don't understand," remarked Savanna.

"I'll be in the audience," Jade resumed, "and when the time is right I'll introduce myself, tell him I'm doing research for my next novel, and establish a connection of mutual interests to further our goal of getting help. It may take a little time but I'll gain his trust and recruit him. It's the only way. Go directly to the source and work from there."

Wolf sat back in his chair and looked at Jade through steepled fingers. Savanna traced Jade's book jacket photo with polished nails while Lucien watched candles throw strange shapes on the barren walls. "Let's take a vote," he mumbled.

Jade's hand flew up in the air but Wolf seemed distracted as if he were listening to a discussion inside his own head. He gripped the arm of his chair. "I don't know brother," he began. "Every encounter we've had with mortals has been detrimental to everyone involved. Why would this be any different?"

"Yeah," Savanna concurred. "I hate the whole ignorant race of greedy leeches."

Jade lowered her hand and slapped the table. "You're forgetting an important detail here. We're in control of this situation. It's our plan, our idea, and our resources. One false move and our new associate will be dead within seconds. The risk is his, not ours, and I say we at least give it a try."

Wolf slowly unfurled his clenched fist and raised his hand. Savanna closed the book and raised hers too. Lucien turned and looked at Jade while lifting his arm. "You're on Jade. Good luck."

A unanimous decision was about to alter the bylaws and history of the Vampire Preservation Society. Mortal and immortal would meet as peers and not prey, allies and not enemies, and healers and not hunters in a quest for survival.

CHAPTER TWENTY-SEVEN

B rown metal folding chairs clanked open as workers set up rows of seats in a spacious auditorium where Dr. Marcus Blackwell would be speaking. Jade arrived early and chose an aisle seat in the first row to the right of the podium. An eclectic group of people, from well-dressed professionals to casually dressed hippies drifted in and settled into neat rows. Both young and old were excited about the doctor's talk and his fundraising efforts to help those who had been stigmatized and ignored for so many years. Jade's blue notebook lay open in her lap, pen poised for notes and a small recorder was tucked in her pocket in case she was able to go through with her plans for a private interview with the good doctor after his lecture.

At seven-thirty p.m. a distinguished looking gentleman entered from a side door and took his a seat at the front of the stage. After a brief introduction Dr. Marcus Blackwell rose, placed his notes on the lectern, and scanned the growing audience with granite gray eyes that almost matched his long silver-streaked ponytail gathered at the nape of his neck. A thin mustache and small white soul patch on his chin framed his dazzling smile and added to his attractiveness and warmth. He seemed approachable, not arrogant, and the joy in his eyes reflected his intent to inform people of how to help AIDS patients often shunned by others.

"Thank you all for coming," he began. "As you know, we have made several positive strides in the fight against AIDS. We acquire more tools each and every day; more information, better ideas, and new resources to help in our fight with the virus. Now, more than ever, we inch closer to finding a cure. We are pioneers on an unknown frontier, explorers in a foreign realm of disease. It is imperative that we continue to fight and conquer AIDS. Our organization is currently applying for grants and research money and with additional funding from you, we can proceed along the path to victory. Thank you for your support!"

The crowd stood and cheered. Blackwell raised his hand and leaned in toward the microphone. "We have prepared a DVD of our research facilities and an overview of our recent projects. After the presentation I will be available for questions."

The lights dimmed and a murmuring crowd sat back in their chairs to watch the video. Jade spotted Blackwell slipping out a side door. She closed her notebook and followed close behind only to find the doctor standing in line at an adjoining coffee shop. Jade grabbed her wallet and approached him with an engaging grin. "Please allow me to buy your coffee Dr. Blackwell. My name is Jade Lee. I'm an author and I find your work fascinating. If you have a moment I'd like to ask you a few quick questions."

Blackwell looked and recognized the petite author. "Ah, Miss Lee, how nice to meet you. I read your last novel and enjoyed it immensely. I've got about twenty minutes until the video is over. I'd be happy to speak with you."

She grabbed his coffee and placed it next to hers on the tray. The cashier rang up the purchase and they found two empty spaces in a small booth near a plant filled window.

"I'm in the process of starting a new novel," Jade said, "and even though it is fiction, it has to be accurate, interesting, and believable. If you don't write with integrity, why bother? I'm considering a character who has contracted AIDS and I would really appreciate some of your input so I can bring my character to life for my readers. Do you have any free time during the evening? I can only imagine how busy you are."

Blackwell glanced at his watch and took a sip of his creamy coffee. "I don't have my appointment book with me, but here's my card. Give my office a call and we'll set something up." He looked at his watch again and got up from his chair. "See you inside," he said walking towards the auditorium. Jade scooped up her purse and notebook and followed close behind.

The next day Jade called Blackwell's office and left a message. Two days later her phone rang at 7:30 a.m. and roused her from a deep sleep. She slept beneath a box spring and mattress in a specially made frame that rolled out from beneath the raised bed. Hidden from view by a long ruffled bed skirt, it was lined with plump silk cushions, a goose down mattress, and a light coverlet that she changed every week to avoid the inevitable boredom that plagued immortals when they tired of the same routines. Unfortunately for her, the sleeping arrangement didn't include soundproofing.

Hissing at the muted sunlight peeking through the edges of heavy dark drapes, she pulled a silk brocade bedspread over her head and listened to the answering machine click on. Blackwell's voice boomed in the quiet room. "This is Marcus Blackwell calling Miss Lee. Sorry for the delay..."

Jade grabbed the phone before he could finish. "Good morning Doctor. How are you?"

"Fine, thanks. I apologize for not calling sooner. I've been out of town fundraising. My schedule is pretty hectic for the next few weeks. Could we meet later this evening for a bite to eat?"

Jade smiled when he used her favorite phrase "bite to eat". She thought for a moment and answered. "Why don't we meet at Witches Brew? Its casual, relaxed, and they have great sandwiches. I'm sure the last thing you want to do is go

someplace formal. Besides, this isn't a technical interview –
more of a conversation about you and your work. How does
8 p.m. sound?"

Blackwell sighed with relief. "OK, no suit and tie required.
Sounds great. I'll see you later tonight."

Jade rolled back under the bed and pulled the covers up to
her chin. No sense in bothering the others right now she
thought as she slipped away into a deep slumber.

CHAPTER TWENTY-EIGHT

A pastel sunset melted into early evening as streetlamps flicked on like fireflies flashing in unison. The light pole outside Jade's cottage beamed down on her iridescent light green Corvette. She trotted to the car and threw her blue-lined steno notebook on the passenger side next to a copy of *Sister Solutions*. She grabbed the book and jotted a few personalized lines to Blackwell and signed it with a flourish. Small price to pay for her interview she thought and turned the key to start the car.

She arrived first and ducked into the ladies room to check her outfit in the mirror. Her jet black hair was pulled back in a ponytail and a large oval citrine dangled from a gold chain around her neck. Her jeans, amber v-neck blouse, and dark brown sweater coat all conveyed a laid back attitude which she hoped would put the doctor at ease.

Marcus entered the restaurant and smiled as soon as he spotted her at a corner table.

"Miss Lee, good to see you again," he said offering his hand.

"The pleasure is mine doctor." She shook his hand, enjoying the warm touch of his fingers on hers. "Have a seat and relax. Sounds like you've been on a whirlwind schedule. I know the feeling. My book tours can be grueling and some fans blur the lines between fantasy and reality and mistake me for one of my characters. Always a fine line between fact and fiction."

Marcus placed his worn briefcase on the floor and glanced around the small café finally looking into Jade's green eyes. He paused for a moment before speaking, a pleasant buzz of attraction tingling in his body, a budding curiosity blossoming in his mind.

"What would you recommend, Miss Lee?"

"Their homemade tuna melt sandwiches are great," she answered, still looking into his twinkling gray eyes. "Fresh raspberry iced tea is always refreshing and sweet potato fries can't be beat," she continued. They placed their orders with a smiling waitress and listened to the soft music drifting through ceiling speakers hidden between fluffy philodendrons and trailing green ivy.

Jade tilted her head and asked, "Do you like jazz Dr. Blackwell or are you more of an opera fan?"

He laughed and sipped from a glass of water. "First off, I like jazz, classic rock, blues, and world music. Second, please call me Marcus. Technically, neither one of us is working so there's no need for formalities. Wouldn't you agree?"

"Only if you call me Jade," she said with a grin.

A pudgy waitress appeared and placed their plates and frosted Mason jar mugs filled with iced tea on the small square yellow Formica table. "Get you anything else?"

"Not right now," they answered in unison. Jade laughed and pulled out her steno pad. She still preferred to take notes the old-fashioned way.

"Ready for a few questions?" she asked. Marcus took a bite out of his sandwich and nodded.

"Can you give me a brief overview of how you chose AIDS as a field of research?"

"Sure. Back in 1981 five young men in California became extremely ill. Two died, and as time passed, more people became sick and modern medicine was introduced to the

AIDS virus. The issue was largely ignored by the Reagan administration. In their estimation only gay men became infected and that mentality fueled a firestorm of homophobia that's still burns today. By the mid 1990's more than half a million people in the United States were diagnosed with AIDS and more than half of those died."

Jade wrote in her notebook and looked up when Blackwell paused. She shared the same compassion for her dying members as he did for the terminally ill patients he spoke of.

"Am I going too fast Miss Lee, I mean Jade?"

She shook her head. "No, please continue."

"After all these years there is still no definitive cure. We've tried protease inhibitors, drug cocktails, and constantly search for new and better ways to deal with the disease and the stigma that goes with it. In an age of instant gratification and ever expanding technologies, simple messages and warnings about AIDS get buried in a maze of complacency and indifference. Here we are in 2015 and CDC estimates show that 1.1 million people in the US are infected and of those, approximately 20% don't even know it! It's more important than ever to keep educating people and to fight this terrible plague. I believe in solutions, not excuses, action, and not denial, and most of all relief from pain and suffering for humankind."

Jade nodded when he finished speaking and closed her notebook. The waitress reappeared and cleared the table. "Dessert?"

"Do you have strawberry shortcake?" Marcus asked.

The waitress smiled and nodded pointing at the picture on the menu.

"One of my favorites," Jade said. "Make it two."

The waitress flipped open her order pad and scratched their order on the paper. "Coming right up."

"Have you always lived here Marcus?" Jade asked switching the focus to a more personal level.

"I grew up in Dorchester, just outside of Boston, a rough neighborhood that can either make you or break you. I got by with some scratches and bruises, shall we say, and put myself through med school with odd jobs and occasional help from my grandparents. I moved to this area a few years ago. I like the option of driving into Boston if I want or going up to Maine for lobster and a bucket of steamers. Kind of centralized here. How about you?"

Jade lowered her eyes before speaking. "I was raised in San Francisco, city by the bay as some like to call it. It's a cold, sometimes dreary place filled with diverse people and a complicated history. After I began my writing career I decided to move east and settled in this area to be near friends. So this is my home base between book tours and writer's conferences."

Dessert arrived and they discussed global warming, environmental concerns, and favorite movies while licking sweet whipped cream and syrupy strawberries from their lips both wondering where this collaboration was going to lead.

CHAPTER TWENTY-NINE

After spending the evening with "the enemy", Jade wanted to share her impressions of him with Savanna despite the fact that her friend despised mortals and viewed them as low-life blood donors unworthy of a second thought. Savanna lived in a small A-frame cottage hugged by fragrant pine trees and sheltered by towering oaks in Rockport, one town over from Gloucester. Lush palm fronds from potted plants framed the entrance to a spacious living room where hand-carved masks, flutes, and colorful hand-woven tapestries hung from the walls. A large bamboo couch and matching chair were filled with soft cushions and toss pillows sheathed in zebra and tiger prints and a large glass coffee table was covered with architectural books, magazines, and an assortment of pencils and other drafting supplies.

To the left of the living room a spiral wrought iron staircase wound its way up to a huge loft where a canopy bed rested against one wall. The bedding matched earth tone drapes that covered the lone window and a large teak armoire took up most of the other side of the room where Savanna slept each night, upright and secured with an inside latch that prevented anyone from opening the doors.

Savanna opened her front door before Jade had stepped

out of her polished Vette.

"I can't wait to hear about the mortal moron," she giggled as soon as Jade reached the doorway. "Come in. I made us a pot of Moringa tea and baked some blood cakes."

Jade grabbed her shoulder bag and threw it on the rug next to the bamboo chair. Fragrant sandalwood incense tickled her nose and a soft dim light shone on the drafting table in the corner.

"Working?" Jade asked kicking off her shoes.

"Yeah, new client. Seems to be open to some of my more daring concepts. Can't stand the ones who want a Frank Lloyd Wright house on a pauper's budget. You know me, I'm happiest when I'm busy."

Jade poured them both a cup of tea and curled up in the comfortable seat. Savanna came out of the kitchen with crimson streaked pink cakes that looked like strawberry muffins.

"So dish! How was your meeting? Is your speaker friend amiable or edible? Testy? Tasty? What gives?"

Jade rolled her eyes and laughed.

"I know how you feel about dealing with mortals this way, but let's make it as painless as possible. I think the way to his head is through his wallet."

Savanna sipped her tea and frowned." What in the world are you talking about, girl? You're beginning to sound like one of them with all your perky puns!"

They both laughed and nibbled on the freshly baked blood cakes.

"Look, we have the same drive to help others. He's highly motivated, focused, and his primary need right now is more funding for research. I think we should present ourselves as philanthropists with considerable resources. Wolf and Lucien can approach him, gain his trust, and when the time is right, we'll take the next step. We have nothing to lose and everything to gain. Worst case scenario is we end up killing him if he becomes a liability and there will be one less mortal in the world."

Savanna laughed again and agreed with her friend. "Sounds like a plan to me, especially the one less mortal part. Yeah, yeah, I know, I'm biased, but I can't help myself. Let's present this to the guys and get on with it. I bet more of us are dying as we speak."

CHAPTER THIRTY

J ade made arrangements for everyone to meet Marcus
Blackwell at a well-known restaurant called The Lobster
Pot where baked stuffed lobster and boiled crab were the
specialties. During her conversation with Marcus she had
learned of his fondness for crustaceans and thought he'd be
more likely to attend a meeting being held where his favorite
food was being served. Unbeknownst to Blackwell, an offer
of funding would accompany dessert, but it would include a
number of stipulations.

Lucien, Wolf, and Savanna joined Jade at an outdoor table
overlooking a short battered pier that stretched out into the
water like a splintered hand grasping for the horizon. Seagulls
swooped in circles screeching for food and colored buoys
bobbed in the rippling waves while a foghorn's loud lament
pierced the evening air. Bright stars lit the sky, a polka dot
coverlet of blue and gold, and everyone agreed it was the best
place to make a generous offer.

They waited nervously for their guest. This would be a
groundbreaking night to be remembered by all throughout the
vampire empire. Negotiations had to be handled with care
and diplomacy. One wrong word or gesture could mean more
unnecessary deaths on both sides.

Lucien and Wolf stood as Dr. Blackwell walked out onto the wooden deck and Jade introduced everyone. They sat opposite each other at the candlelit table and Wolf sat at the end tucked in near Lucien and Savanna. A young waiter with slicked back hair and tiny hoop earrings took their drink orders and promptly returned with a tray filled with four Bloody Marys and a Perrier and lime. Everyone sipped for a moment, glancing at the menu and deciding what to order. Lucien broke the awkward silence by starting a conversation about their varied occupations.

"I'm an art historian," Lucien said, handing Marcus a slick multi-colored business card. "I work closely with museums and private collectors interested in restoration, appraisals, buying, selling – I'm sure you get the idea. Renoir and Monet are my personal favorites and I enjoy sharing my insights with those who appreciate fine art," he added with a smile.

Savanna presented her card next. "I'm an architect and I dabble in graphic arts sometimes. Pleased to meet you."

Marcus glanced at the navy blue business card and smiled. "You must enjoy working with the new solar energy concepts and designs," he said amiably.

"Not a big fan," Savanna answered dryly. "I try to incorporate a bit of myself into everything I do. My goal is to please the client and satisfy the inner craving I have for personal satisfaction. Rather symbiotic, don't you think Dr. Blackwell? I help you, you help me. The trick is to anticipate and participate, see the need and finish the deed."

Wolf cleared his throat and kicked Savanna's shoe under the table. It was hard enough reading a mortal above the constant hum of chattering diners and the occasional whiff of blood rare beef made him grind his teeth in exasperation.

"My specialty is Native American artifacts," Wolf explained. "I work as an independent consultant to assist with various projects such as the Native American Graves Protection and Repatriation Act to help maintain the integrity and sacredness of my people's culture and beliefs. My friends know how to reach me if the need arises. I don't have a card

108

but offer you a small river stone as a token of my appreciation for all living things."

Marcus held the pebble in the palm of his hand and put the business cards in the inside pocket of his suit jacket. He looked across the table at Jade and smiled.

"You already know what I do Marcus," Jade said mirroring his smile. "I'm flattered that you're familiar with my work and grateful that you accepted our invitation for dinner. We have a few things we'd like to discuss with you after dinner."

His eyes softened when he glanced at Jade and the corners of his mouth twitched with unspoken compliments. As if on cue, dishes clinked, silverware clattered, and four servings of bloody rare beef and a lone stuffed lobster were spread out on the table. It was difficult for all four leaders to keep their fangs concealed but napkins and frequent bites of warm bread helped.

Eventually the talk evolved from light conversational subjects to more serious topics such as the spread of AIDS, lack of research funds, and the determination of medical personnel intent on finding a cure. They all ordered tiramisu for dessert and while they waited for the coffee-flavored treat, Jade slid a large white envelope across the table to Marcus. Puzzled, he picked it up and looked at his companions.

"We believe in you and your work Marcus," Jade said softly. "Please accept this and any future contributions as a token of our appreciation. We all believe that safeguarding the human race is of paramount importance. The efforts of a few will benefit the whole and one voice in the darkness might illuminate the way for others to follow."

Marcus tucked the envelope into his briefcase and shook everyone's hand. ""I'm very grateful for your support and am delighted that you share my enthusiasm and passion for finding a cure. My office will be in touch with you so that we may properly acknowledge your gift."

Lucien stole a glance at Jade then smiled at Marcus over the rim of his wine glass. "We prefer to remain anonymous, if you don't mind Dr. Blackwell. Too much notoriety is counterproductive. We have more funds at our disposal and look forward to hearing about your results. Unfortunately I have an important conference call scheduled in half an hour and must leave. Our group will be in touch. Goodnight, Dr. Blackwell, it's been a pleasure."

Wolf and Savanna murmured their goodnights and Jade walked Marcus to his white SUV in the corner of the parking lot.

"I'll call you at the end of the week," Jade said demurely as he opened his door and placed his briefcase on the passenger side seat.

"Sounds good," he said, winking and checking his rear view mirror. "Have a good night Jade."

He drove off and Jade jumped into her gleaming green Vette, taillights torching the darkness, purring engine lulling the world back to sleep. She wondered if he'd open the envelope tonight or leave it tucked inside his briefcase with all the other papers. Only time would tell. She shifted gears and cruised around town looking for a hot-blooded meal.

On the other side of town Marcus stepped inside his condo, loosened his tie, and grabbed a tall glass of iced water before turning on the local news. The anchor person droned on about an accident on the highway, the change in weather, and previewed an upcoming story on an injured sports player. Bored and a bit restless, he opened his briefcase and reached for the envelope containing a contribution from his new benefactors.

The shiny silver letter opener slit through the paper with ease and Blackwell grabbed the check before it fluttered to the floor. He read the amount, shook his head as if to clear it, and then held the piece of paper under the lampshade to get a better look. The room and all his surroundings became a distant blur and he felt dizzy and giddy at the same time. He needed to sit and his body seemed to move in slow motion as he headed for the couch.

The check was for five million dollars, the largest amount he had ever received from a single donor. Gratitude replaced disbelief, relief tugged at the corners of his mind and trickled into his limbs as he came to the realization that he was one step closer to fulfilling his dreams.

CHAPTER THIRTY-ONE

During the next month numerous sectors continued to report a decline in population. Many vampires wanted to de-regulate re-births, hoping they could replace the voids left by the newly deceased. Loud arguments and fights broke out at several meetings and some members wondered who was in charge of the on-going investigation. Unbeknownst to anyone, the rings and ash were under lock and key at Nightshade Manor where Lucien allowed Hobo to monitor the collection knowing he would do his best to impress the others once they found out he was in charge.

In the meantime, Jade received approval from the others to continue screening Dr. Blackwell as a potential ally for their cause. She hoped to learn more about him and his research findings before actually revealing their hidden agenda. She picked up her cell and spoke into the receiver. "Call Blackwell at home." The numbers clicked through and the phone rang on the other end.

"Marcus, it's Jade," she said, disappointed that his answering machine had picked up. "I was hoping I could get a copy of your speaking engagement schedule so that I..."

"Hi Jade, I'm here," he answered. "I just got out of the shower and heard your voice. How are you? How's the book coming along?"

Jade smiled at the sound of his voice and grabbed a pen and a piece of paper.

"I'm fine Marcus. About the book. I need a few more details. Would it be possible for me to attend a few of your fundraisers to take notes, ask a few questions, and observe your audience? It would really help as my preference is to draw on personal experiences whenever I can. Being an audience member would give me a unique perspective into the whole process."

Blackwell grinned, pleased at the prospect of spending more time with the attractive author. "Speaking of fundraising, you are your partners were most generous with your donation. I'm still absorbing the fact that I now have funds available for additional testing and have the ability to make substantial contributions to the eradication of the AIDS virus. It would be my pleasure to have you accompany me to events. Most of my engagements are local although I may have one or two out of state. In fact, this Tuesday I have to I have a fundraising luncheon at noon in Portsmouth, New Hampshire. Care to join me?"

Caught off guard by his invitation for a day trip, she feigned disappointment. "Oh, sorry Marcus, I'm booked solid that day, meetings with my agent, editor, all that kind of stuff. Evenings work best for me. Better yet, how would you like a home cooked meal for a change? You could bring a copy of your schedule, we could discuss breakthroughs in science, and perhaps get to know each other a little better."

A warm flush crept up Blackwell's neck and dusted his cheeks with a rose-tinted blush like a schoolboy who just shared his first kiss with a pretty girl. He flipped open his iPad and checked the date on his calendar.

"How about 8p.m. on Thursday night?"

"Looking forward to it. See you then, doc."

Thursday night arrived and with it came an unusual sense of self-consciousness. It had been so long since Jade had prepared real human food she had forgotten how. She

113

refreshed her memory on the Internet and tested each appliance several times so she could appear to know what she was doing. A simple meal of steak, salad, corn on the cob, and baked potatoes seemed easy enough and remembering the doctor's fondness for dessert, she bought the ingredients for fresh strawberry shortcake. Before fumbling around in the kitchen she pulled out her DVD of *Shadow of the Vampire* starring Willem Dafoe as a real vampire playing a vampire in the making of the 1922 film *Nosferatu*. Great film and a good ice breaker she reasoned.

At precisely 8 p.m. the doorbell rang. Jade smoothed her hair, opened the door, and found Marcus standing on her small patio, flowers in one hand, a bottle of wine in the other, and a radiant smile beaming across his face. He wore jeans, a light blue shirt, and a pair of well-worn polished brown cowboy boots. Jade thought he gave new meaning to the term eye-candy.

"Come in, welcome to my writer's retreat also known as the home of my tomes. The flowers are lovely. I'll put them in water while you make yourself at home."

Marcus sat on the couch and looked around at the books lining the walls in pyramid shaped bookcases and hand-painted wooden crates. Reams of unopened paper were neatly stacked by the desk and a modem and router blinked on top of a small cabinet beneath a stained glass window. At the top of each wall in every room were a series of Chinese symbols which seemed to be more than just decorative designs.

"Nice place you have here Jade, away from the crowds and traffic of the city. Very peaceful and serene."

She handed him a glass of wine and sat down beside him. "Thanks. I'm somewhat of a hermit, most writers are solitary by nature and I like the quiet when I'm writing, no distractions or surprises. Dinner is almost ready. I hope you brought your appetite. I know I did," she said coyly.

She refilled their wine glasses, adding a few drops of refrigerated pig blood to hers, and sat down to eat at a small circular table. Jade watched the doctor's hands as he gestured and tore apart a soft dinner roll, placing the buttered biscuit between soft lips that she wanted to lick and maybe kiss. She gazed into his eyes and listened as he spoke of childhood dreams and adult accomplishments and then asked her about her life and the journeys she'd been on. After a flirtatious dessert of strawberries and whipped cream they moved back to the couch and settled in to watch the movie. Jade pressed the buttons on her remote control and the flat screen TV flickered to life.

"I hope you like vampire movies Marcus."

He put his arm around her and squeezed. "Don't worry, I'll protect you," he answered in a B-movie voice.

A strange yearning stirred inside her, a feeling in the pit of her stomach, vaguely familiar but disquieting nonetheless. Pulsing carotid arteries danced above the starched collar on the mortal's shirt and she could hear the faint sound of warm blood gushing through the arteries and veins encased in his muscular frame. Human scents teased her nostrils making her body tingle and her mind roam. She rested her head on his shoulder and listened to the rhythmic beating of his heart beckoning, urging, pulling her to touch, feel, and taste him right there on the couch. She cried out, shocked at the realization that she craved his blood yet lusted for his body.

"Jade, we don't have to watch this if it bothers you," Marcus said gently, mistaking her outburst as a sign of cinematic fear.

"No, Marcus, I'm ok. Really I am."

She got up and poured more wine adding more blood to hers to calm the turbulent churning inside. She sat and Marcus pulled her close, his lips mere inches from hers. Raw primal hunger surged through her shredding her senses and drenching her mind. She had to decide, foreplay or foul play, a kiss or a bite? Her fangs chafed against the soft inside of her upper lip and her mouth quivered longing for a taste, a gush, a long drink of hot surging blood. Feed or fornicate? Caress or kill? She nuzzled his neck, felt his soft hair brush against her cheek. She opened her mouth, tongue quivering in anticipation, and was ready to make a move.

A pounding knock on the door startled the both of them. Jade jumped up, straightened her clothes and smoothed back her hair, annoyed at the interruption. Peeking through closed curtains she saw Savanna standing under the light, arms crossed, a glowering look on her usually calm face.

"Excuse me a minute Marcus. It's Savanna. Must be important." She stepped outside into the cool night air and inhaled the fresh scent of night blooming jasmine.

"What the hell do you think you're doing?" hissed Savanna. "I can't believe it! You almost ate the one person who may be able to help us! What is wrong with you?"

"How did you know?" Jade asked puzzled.

"Are you kidding? That kind of conflicted intensity has a life of its own. I could feel you all the way across town, girl!"

Jade pulled Savanna away from the house. "I know what it looks like, really I do. But that's not what was happening. I don't know how to explain it. I wanted him, yes, but not just in the usual way. I wanted every part of him, like humans do, I'm ashamed to say. Something happened and I felt like a teenage mortal, hormonal and horny. I'm so glad you stopped us! There's no telling where that could have gone."

The door opened and Marcus poked his head out. "Everything alright?"

Savanna glanced at the doctor and smirked. "Yeah, everything is fine. I lost my appointment book and thought I left it here. Couldn't reach Jade on her cell phone so I decided to swing by. Sorry for disturbing you two."

Marcus smiled and placed his hand on Jade's shoulder. "I've got some early appointments in the morning and really need to be going. Thanks for dinner, it was great. I'll be in touch." He winked and gave her a kiss on the cheek.

Savanna left, too, and Jade cleared the table and cleaned the kitchen. Close call she thought crawling underneath the mattresses to reach her bed. Got to re-evaluate my strategy with the appetizing doctor she mused before drifting off to sleep.

CHAPTER THIRTY-TWO

More copper rings were added to the pile locked in the vault at Nightshade Manor. Hobo kept count and polished the rings every night while the leaders took care of other concerns. Lucien spent time with Lucas sharing happy boyhood memories and Wolf was in Southern Oregon identifying some Native remains that had recently been found beneath a grove of felled trees. Savanna was at a geodesic dome workshop in New Mexico discussing the advantages of solar living and Jade took advantage of some quiet time to catch up on her work.

Early one evening, just before the sun began its slow descent into the dusky horizon, Jade sat at her kitchen table looking at spreadsheets detailing the weekly loss of members in her sector. The doorbell rang startling her from deep concentration and breaking her train of thought. It was late afternoon, everyone was gone, and she wasn't expecting any visitors so she didn't answer. Next a light rapping on the door caught her attention and she peeked through the heavy drapes and was surprised to see Marcus standing at the door with a folder tucked under his arm and a cell phone clutched in his hand.

She cracked the door open, careful not to let any streaming sunbeams hit her snow-white skin. "Marcus, what a surprise!"

He peered at her through long lashes and smiled. "I tried calling first but your phone went right to voicemail. I just got back to town and wanted to give you a copy of my new itinerary, if you're still interested."

"Sure. Please, come in."

Marcus glanced at the papers strewn across the table and hesitated before going any further. "Are you writing? I can come back later."

Now is the time to tell him she thought to herself. I can't keep putting this off. The situation is getting worse and we're desperate for help.

"Can we talk Marcus? There's something important I need to tell you. Would you like some coffee or tea or a glass of wine?"

He settled into the couch. "Nothing thanks. I'm fine. If it's about my last time here ..."

She took his hand in hers and placed it gently on her thigh. "Do you remember the movie we watched?"

"The vampires? Good movie. What about it?"

She closed her eyes and steeled herself for rejection, horror, and possible clinical observation by the only mortal she ever felt a true connection to. Greater good, greater good, she repeated over and over in her scrambled mind.

"Uh, Marcus, there's no easy way to say this. I have to show you. Do you have a stethoscope with you?"

A frown creased his forehead and a look of concern washed over his face. "Jade if you're sick I'll help in any way I can. Let me get my bag." He jumped up and headed for the door.

Stray sunbeams from the setting sun poked through a lattice fence running along the side of her dirt driveway. On impulse, she pushed Marcus aside and ran out the door.

"I'll get it! I'll get it!" she yelled racing toward Blackwell's SUV. A patch of fading sunlight hit her forearm as she reached into the backseat and tiny sparks of flames and wisps of chalky smoke danced along her arm like laser beams gone awry. Marcus stared in horror as she howled in agony and raced across the walkway to carry her inside.

"I'll get some ice," he stuttered heading towards the kitchen. He opened the freezer door and gasped. Pouches of frozen blood were piled neatly, one on top of the other, inside the spacious freezer. Each bag was labeled with a date and marked "pig", "cow", or "human." He pulled the refrigerator door open and gaped at several containers of Hemo-Sip, real human blood, and packages of raw beef liver.

"What the hell..." He turned and stared at Jade's mouth. Two glistening fangs sparkled like falling stars in a midnight sky and her eyes gleamed with pink-tinged tears.

"This is what I've been trying to tell you! I'm a vampire and I need your help! Please listen to me! I need to explain!"

Marcus stumbled and fell onto the carpeted floor. His hands trembled and beads of perspiration trickled down his neck and soaked the underarms of his shirt and chest. Too stunned to move, he leaned back and rested his head on the polished door frame.

Jade crawled over to him, looked deeply into the shocked man's eyes, and caressed his warm face with cool satiny fingers to help soothe his riled state of mind. She took his sweaty palm and placed it on her chest where her mortal heart ceased to beat so many years ago.

"I no longer have a pulse but I do have a conscience. My people have watched and learned from yours over the centuries and have seen the consequences of your actions. Global warming, fracking, worldwide hunger, GMOS, the list goes on and on and now we face contaminated food sources that are threatening our whole species. I, we, need your help, Marcus. This is a catastrophe in the making, the likes of which we've never seen, and it will affect your kind as well. Please hear us out," she pleaded.

Somewhere outside cats screeched and dogs barked in a battle between two separate species that was mirrored inside the small home.

"Why me?" he asked incredulously. "There are others? Where are they? Who are they? What does this mean? What

119

do you want from me? Did you hand me an automatic death sentence by telling me all this? I don't understand!"

Jade's enthusiasm evaporated into a strange sense of sadness. She hadn't realized the enormity of what she was trying to do getting a mortal, especially a doctor, to fully grasp the illogical concept of immortality. It was different for her; she directly experienced the conversion from living to undead. His angst and pain added to her growing fondness for him and things were becoming a bit more complicated.

"I would never hurt you Marcus. I consider you a friend, but I must insist that you keep this conversation between the two of us secret, otherwise I'll have no choice and I'll be forced to kill you."

Marcus nodded, too astonished to speak, and grabbed his keys walking out the door without looking back.

CHAPTER THIRTY-THREE

The following night everyone met at Jade's cottage by 8 p.m. prepared for the worst but hoping for help. After Marcus left the night before, she called everyone and informed them that, in an act of desperation, she had revealed her immortality to him. Concerned that he might decide to cut off communication she had taken advantage of his disheveled state of mind and hid his cell phone and wallet. A frantic phone call from him early that morning guaranteed his presence at the cottage that night and she was truly anxious to see him.

The group chatted quietly waiting for Marcus to arrive and when the headlights appeared at the top of the driveway they looked at each other as a gesture of support. Marcus knocked and entered looking pale and drawn. He wanted to gather his belongings and leave but the sight of his new investors gathered around the room forced him to reconsider.

He glanced at Jade and shrugged. "Is this some kind of joke? Is there a hidden camera somewhere recording my reactions to your clever hoax? That check you gave me has been cashed and is real so I don't see the point in prolonging this charade any longer. Can I get my phone and wallet, please, and I'll be on my way."

"Dr. Blackwell," Savanna said, reaching for the sandalwood

box she had carried in from her car. "This container holds the remains of our once immortal friends. I know we are pushing the limits of your patience and the boundaries of credibility but we are desperate. We are vampires and members of our race are suffering painful deaths, crumbling to ash and grit, and your infected people are dying, too! We want to see if there is a connection between your AIDS virus and whatever is killing our members. Can you help us?"

Blackwell slowly raised the rectangular lid of the box and peered inside. Several copper rings in baggies were covered in a substance that looked like blue powder. He glanced at Lucien hoping for an explanation. Lucien met his gaze and spoke in a low tone. "You are looking at the remains of some of our brethren. It's all we have to work with. Immortality granted us freedom from disease and death until now. There's never been a need for doctors or medical care of any kind. One of our members who dropped out of med school when he joined our clan has studied the blue ash and believes there is a possibility that a mortal virus has somehow mutated and enhanced its ability to cross into our genetic material via direct contact. Our physiology changes once we cross the line into immortality but our instinct for survival and preservation doesn't. We need your help, Dr. Blackwell, and we're prepared to assist you in any way we can."

Blackwell opened one of the baggies and pinched a small amount of blue ash between his thumb and forefinger. Bright blue residue formed imprints on the tips of his fingers and he thought of all the AIDS victims whose remains lay buried in coffins or rested in cherished cremation urns mourned and missed for years to come. The four vampires watched him carefully close the box.

"We represent the four races of humanity," Wolf added. "Each of us was mortal at one time and were specially chosen to receive the gift of eternal life so that we could protect, preserve, and honor all cultures throughout the world. Your rational mind may not accept what we are saying but if you listen with your heart, you will hear what we are saying."

Fear, sadness, and empathy washed over Blackwell as he listened. "I need some time alone to think and weigh out some options. I'll be back in touch in a few days." He stood, shook hands with the nocturnal group, and put his belongings in his pocket. Jade took his arm and walked him to the door.

"Marcus, if you choose not to help, please respect our need for privacy. We've risked everything tonight just by speaking with you. The virus is not our only enemy. You mortals have spun diabolical stories about us for centuries. Despite what you may think, we are not all evil. We do what we need to survive and it is beyond our abilities to change that. Please consider our request carefully."

CHAPTER THIRTY-FOUR

Raindrops pelted the windshield of his SUV as Marcus drove to his condo perched on a hilltop near the center of town. Twinkling lights from the buildings and homes below filled his bay window like fireflies flitting in moonbeams. He sat on the edge of his bed listening to the rain pound the windowpanes like tiny drummers in a marching band.

His head throbbed, a mixture of pain and tension intertwined. Was this all a joke? Did they get paid to perform in some type of video lunacy? Will I look like an idiot? Did I say anything stupid? I'll call Jade tomorrow and congratulate her on her acting skills. Her friends were good, too. He walked to the bathroom, took some ibuprofen, and rested his head on a plump feather pillow, finally drifting off to sleep with one last thought running through his mind. But what if...?

Jogging along the circular path around Ives Park, Marcus noticed a small black cat peeking out between the rusted rungs of an old wooden bench. He continued to trot, mentally planning his schedule for the day. Sunday was his relaxation day. He liked to think of it as Funday, twenty-four hours of rest and relaxation.

   While on the next lap, the cat jumped onto the path in front of him, its emerald eyes begging for contact, and its mews a plea for attention. Captivated by the feline's stare, Marcus bent down to pat it. He felt the claws first, digging into the soft flesh of his eyelids and raking small burrows in his cheeks. The wriggling body felt enormous. Salty tears streaked his face and bloody scratches burned like fire. The cat growled in his ear and shredded the soft skin on his neck with giant fangs, slashing his carotid artery and sending shards of pain into his chest and shoulder. He reached out to grab the scruff of his attacker's neck only to find blue ash drifting between his fingers. Helpless and alone, he laid on the cold damp ground touching the darkened circle of blood congealing beneath his ear. With each beat of his heart he felt the life being pumped out of his body like a flattened tire poked with a rusted nail. His heartbeat slowed and grew faint, like the wings of a fledgling bird learning how to fly and his shallow breaths barely filled his lungs. He was alone and dying; no one to help, no breath left to cry out for help, just a loud buzzing that sounded like swarming cicadas. Slowly he rolled his blood soaked head to one side and saw four luminous numbers flashing in the dark.

   Jolted from sleep, Marcus awoke from the worst nightmare of his life. He hit the snooze button and reveled in the realization that he wasn't really dying. He looked at his hands remembering the feel of blue ash dusting his fingertips like silken powder and decided not to dismiss the vampire claims.

CHAPTER THIRTY-FIVE

While the leaders scurried around taking care of their business matters, Hobo enjoyed his newfound notoriety as Lucien's assistant. It seemed to him that other vampires were more respectful and some went out of their way to stop by his office to say hello. Someday I'll be in the inner circle he thought and I'll be able to spend more time with Lucien. The adoration he felt for his mentor bordered on obsession and he resented the fact that for some strange reason, Marcus Blackwell required more attention from all four leaders.

Several weeks had passed and the only progress being made was the addition of more copper rings to the pile. It occurred to Hobo early one evening, when everyone was scattered to parts unknown, that he could outshine the mortal doctor and find a cure of the new illness by himself and become Lucien's best friend in the process. It didn't matter that he had no medical training and barely squeaked by in high school biology class. He could use whatever means he had at his disposal, whether it be Wiccan, paranormal, or plain old hippie ingenuity. He was, after all, the only one Lucien trusted enough to watch over the magical jewelry, the real keys to the future. The secret was in the rings, he was sure of it. If he could manipulate the mysterious components of the copper rings, maybe he could save the all vampires and sire a whole new generation of inoculated immortals!

The most logical step was to contact a metallurgist to find out the properties of copper and its alloys. He sighed. Sometimes mortals were a necessary evil. He decided to look up Nik Stevens, his old friend from Woodstock days. After their fate-filled journey to New York, Nickel went on to become a silversmith and metal sculptor whose hand-crafted items were sold in tourist havens throughout New England. His unique designs and talent were well-known locally and his preference for solitude added an aura of mystery to his artistic persona.

Hobo grabbed a phone book and thumbed through the pages. He disliked the new-fangled contraptions like laptops and tablets and didn't know how to use any of them. Besides, he always said, tablets are for taking when you're sick, not for pounding with your fingers when you need something. He found Nik's number, poked the keypad on his flip phone and pressed the send button. After a few clicks and ringing noises his old friend answered.

"Hey, Nickel my man, its Hobo, uh, I mean Jonathan Green. Remember me?"

The sound of clanking machinery in the background almost drowned out Nickel's voice. "Hold on a minute. Let me turn this off." The line went silent and Hobo wasn't sure if they were disconnected or if his friend had hung up. A few seconds later a raspy voice answered.

"How could I forget you dude! You left me stranded at Woodstock and I had to hitchhike home with a hog farmer who made me sit in the back of his pickup with a bunch of shit spewing squealing piglets who never shut up! To this day I don't eat pork and still curse you out every time I see that Woodstock movie on TV. How the hell are ya Jonathan?"

Jonathan laughed, pinkish tears rolling down his face as he pictured the mobile pig sty ride. "Sorry about that. I went on a different kind of trip but more about that later. You can call me Hobo and I'll add that story to the mix, too. Can you meet me for a beer somewhere near Buzzards Bay about 8:30 tomorrow night?"

"Sure. Which bar?"

"How about the Trippy Hippy?"

"Know it well. See you then. Later, buddy."

Hobo went back to his room near the vault and went over the crude flowchart he had drawn on the back of a cardboard incense box. He lit a stick of patchouli, placed it in his walking stick, and considered his plan. It looked good on paper and made sense in his head, but the question was how much should he reveal to a fading mortal. Back in the day they trusted each other like brothers but time had a way of changing people, some more than others. He finally decided a few brews would make a difference in how to handle the whole thing.

The next night Hobo grabbed a quick meal beneath the Bourne Bridge and made his way to the bar. He entered the Trippy Hippy and spotted Nickel right away. His old partying pal looked pretty much the same except for the inevitable signs of mortal aging. His long, white frizzy hair was pulled back into a scraggly ponytail and blue tinted granny glasses rested on his thin, beaklike nose.

"Hey, Green, over here!" he yelled, waving his navy blue Red Sox hat in the air. "Take a load off." Hobo ambled over and took a seat.

"Damn! Look at you Jonathan, I mean Hobo. You haven't changed one bit since the last time I saw you. What did you do? Discover the fountain of youth?"

Hobo hadn't considered his youthful appearance when hatching his plan and his mind raced to come up with a plausible explanation.

"Good living, my man, that and some mighty good weed. Slows everything down, if you catch my drift," he chuckled.

Both men laughed and ordered a pitcher of beer from the frowning waitress. The bar was only half full at this time of night and crossing over the threshold was like taking a step back in time. A huge psychedelic peace sign flashed on the wall between both restrooms and framed posters of Hendrix, Joplin, and The Doors lined the sheetrock walls. A couple of middle aged men played pool on a worn pool table and an old jukebox loaded with 45 rpm records blasted classic rock tunes from glowing neon speakers. Time may have stood still here, thought Hobo, feeling a bit wistful and nostalgic, and so have I.

After a few frosty mugs of ale Hobo listened intently as his pal brought him up to date on the changes in their old neighborhood, the deaths of old friends, and the many disadvantages of growing older while feeling quite young. His physical form may have changed but Nik Stevens was still a free spirit at heart and Hobo remembered why they had been such good friends all those years ago.

"So what have you been up to?" Nickel asked, munching on stale peanuts and chewy popcorn.

Hobo glanced around to see if anyone was nearby, then took a deep breath.

"You wouldn't believe me if I told you. Let's just say I'm living an alternative lifestyle and it will become more apparent as time goes on."

Jim Morrison belted out "People Are Strange" on the jukebox and someone yelled for another beer. Nickel looked at his friend, wiggled his eyebrows up and down, and giggled.

"Are you telling me you've gone over to the other side? An alternative lifestyle like in San Francisco or Provincetown?"

Hobo laughed and put his mug on the table. "No, not that kind of change. Let me put it this way. I've had a chance to expand my horizons, in more ways than one, and an opportunity has arisen which requires your knowledge and my ideas. If you think you might be interested let me know. I'll supply the materials and you provide the craftsmanship. What do you think?"

Nickel blinked a couple of times and burped. "Ok good buddy. Can't wait to hear what you got in mind. I'm still a bit confused about your alternative lifestyle and all that but as long as I don't have to eat any fruits, nuts, or tofu crap I'm game."

Hobo hugged his friend and smiled. "It may involve some dietary changes but not right away. Go home and crash. I'll call you later this week."

CHAPTER THIRTY-SIX

Hobo noticed that the fine blue ash clung to everything it came in contact with. Dark blue vials were used for storing the vampire remains to minimize exposure to sources that might contaminate or degrade the valuable dust. Each container was securely fastened with rubberized caps to prevent accidental leakage and bright yellow labels were marked with the date, location of discovery, identity of the finder, and the victim's name if known. Guarding the ashes and rings gave Hobo a sense of purpose and was a source of great pride. Lucien must really trust me, he thought. He only checks in for periodic updates. He must know I'm doing a good job.

For several nights in a row Hobo drew diagrams and endless flowcharts to try to figure out a formula that would protect everyone from the blue death via new copper rings. The secret magic ingredients couldn't be duplicated or extracted from the original rings so he had to use some from the pile if his idea was going to work. He had already skimmed blue ash from several vials and he had it tucked away in his leather backpack. "The prototype must be carefully tested," he mumbled, "and the first batch of rings must be small in quantity, but very high quality or the master plan won't work. Each piece has to be indistinguishable from

131

the original and still be easy to place on a newborn vampire's quivering hand."

Nickel and Hobo met a few nights later in a small shack behind Nickel's house near Carver, Massachusetts. A strong breeze rattled a lone light bulb suspended from the ceiling and two cats snarled at each other in a battle over foraged food. Burn marks etched the edge of a cluttered worktable like singed fringe and tools hung from painted pegboards like metal sentinels waiting for commands. Hobo tapped his foot on an old welcome mat and felt like a little kid on Christmas Eve. His big project was about to be unveiled.

He spread the papers across the table and pointed at some figures and shapes on the first sheet of paper. "Nickel, my man, you are looking at a formula that will revolutionize history and make us both famous. The importance of this new product cannot be underestimated. I'm putting all my trust in you. Once you look it all over and figure out your part of the equation, I'll explain how important everything is."

Nickel pushed the brim of his Red Sox hat off his forehead and scratched his ear. Nothing looked particularly important or even interesting to him for that matter.

"Have you had a few too many old friend?" he asked. "I mean its okay. Really. A few burnt brain cells never hurt a boy much, and after all, we are 'children of the 60's' as they say. We're entitled to a certain amount of burn out. Know what I mean?"

Hobo rolled his bloodshot eyes and pointed to the clock. "Call me when you have something. Follow the directions exactly as I've written them. I can guarantee that you will be one helluva happy hippie by the time I get through with you."

"Promises, promises," Nickel muttered under his breath, skimming the papers with tired, strained eyes.

CHAPTER THIRTY-SEVEN

A cross town Lucas became increasingly involved in the blue ash crisis. He spoke regularly with Lucien who kept him abreast of current developments and they both enjoyed their new bond. While the others tended to their business affairs, Lucas worked on finding an all-natural, plant based cure using the extensive network of contacts he had made with his LL Greens line of supplements. He named the new project *Super Natural Solutions* or SNS for short.

Over the years Lucas had studied the subject of ethnobotany and wondered if the spiritual and medicinal properties of such plants as psilocybin, peyote, or ayahuasca could lead to a cure. He considered the idea that the correct dosage, combined with other natural ingredients, might further enhance vampiric perceptions and give them an increased awareness of tainted food sources. After careful consideration he decided against that avenue of research. There were too many variables to take into consideration and he didn't want to further deplete any of the dwindling natural resources that mortals continued to plunder.

After his last talk with Lucien, Lucas converted his small basement into a makeshift lab. His years of formulating supplements for humans gave him easy access to medical supplies and specialized software programs. The biggest dilemma for him on this night was whether to find a way to inoculate humans to protect immortal food sources or to develop an immunization program for vampires as a preventative measure against diseased humans.

A variety of flasks, vials, and eye droppers were neatly tucked into a large plastic container next to two small mice housed in separate cages. He watched the tiny rodents spinning inside their metal exercise wheels like whirring blades in a blender then jotted two names on hot pink sticky notes and taped the paper to the top of each cage. "I hereby christen you Bad and Vlad."

Lucas glanced at his watch, noted the date and time, and scratched some computations onto the lined pages of his notebook. He still preferred to work on paper rather than a calculator or laptop screen. He believed it gave him an edge over the techno-types who couldn't do anything without consulting an app. He removed a small syringe from a sealed package and stuck it in his arm to withdraw a small amount of his blood. He opened the vial and sprinkled a pinch of blue ash, some medicinal herbs, and a few drops of his liquefied supplements and placed the mixture into a centrifugal mixer for a few minutes before drawing the finished product back up into another syringe.

Next he opened the cage, grabbed Vlad by the tail, and injected the squirming creature with the green-tinged concoction. He placed the dosed mouse back in the cage and switched the overhead light off. "It's my dinnertime, mini-mice, and I need to eat before you become appetizers. See you in a few hours." He locked the basement door and let his predatory skills lead him to a warm nutritious meal.

He returned home about an hour before dawn, belly full of warm blood and mind blazing with curiosity. He hurried downstairs to check on his tiny test subjects and was surprised by what he found. Vlad, the world's first immortally modified mouse, had chewed through both metal cages and his partner Bad lay dead on his side with two small puncture wounds visible on his neck. Vlad snored gently beside the stiffened

134

carcass.

Lucas scooped the groggy mouse into his hands and peered into its beady eyes. "End of the line for you pal. Last thing I need is for someone to accuse me of creating a Franken mouse." With the flick of his wrist he snapped the creature's neck and skewered it with a ballpoint pen. "Better stick with Petri dishes," he muttered as he headed upstairs for bed.

CHAPTER THIRTY-EIGHT

While Nickel worked his smelting magic with the stolen copper rings, Hobo stayed busy cleaning the storage room at the castle and marking entries in the death log whenever Lucien called them in. He waited patiently for several days and then paid Nickel a visit in the drafty shack.

Shafts of light poked out from splintered planks of wood and Hobo heard the faint sound of a classic rock tune drifting through the foggy night air. He peered through a grimy window and caught the glint of a pile of copper rings stacked in a fishing tackle box next to an unplugged soldering iron.

"Show me the money!" he spouted entering the room like a gale force wind.

Nickel jumped and dropped a lit joint on the floor. "You scared the shit out of me, man! What money?"

Hobo leaned over, picked up the joint, took a hit and handed it to Nickel. "That's a line from one of your mort, uh, I mean movie stories. Never mind."

The rings seemed to shimmer like heat on a scorched desert highway simmering in noon day sun. Unable to resist, Hobo reached for a ring and held it in the palm of his hand. There was no way to tell if this was one of the original pieces or an imitation. "Nickel, which is which? You did such a good

136

job even I can't tell."

The beaming jeweler pointed towards a small cardboard box next to his tools. "I saved a couple of originals in there. The ones you're holding are my creations, made to your exact specifications. Now, will you tell me what the hell is going on?"

Hobo sniffed the air like a hungry coyote in search of food. Humans had a curious scent, a mix of soap, sweat, and a sprinkle of subtle fear that lay beneath the surface of their greedy souls and he needed to be sure he could speak freely.

"Here's the deal," he began. "Wait, got any beer? Better yet, you might need some Jack Daniels to handle this little bombshell I'm about to drop."

"I'll stick with my Bud, thanks. Need to keep my wits about me. Let's get on with it!"

The wind picked up and the din of metallic wind chimes clanged in bare tree branches outside the rickety door. "These rings are the admission tickets to a whole new way of life filled with eternal peace and love. Real circles of life, man! Remember when I dropped out of sight after the concert? I had no choice! I'm a vampire, Nickel, and I was reborn at Woodstock. I travel at night and eat all kinds of things, dogs, cats, possums, pretty much anything with warm blood except armadillos – too much work for me. I settled here for awhile and was appointed special assistant to one of the big wigs in the organization. We're having some problems and you've solved them all with these custom rings."

Nickel laughed, tears streaming down his face fogging his blue granny glasses. He stood, wiped them with a corner of his torn tie dyed tee shirt and pushed them back on his nose still laughing at Hobo's story.

"What the hell are you on? Shrooms? Acid? Some kind of other weird shit I don't know about? And, more important, got anymore?"

It took Hobo a few moments to realize that his mortal friend wasn't taking him seriously. Time is wasting, time for tasting he thought.

"Nik, look at me and listen to what I'm saying. You'll have the best high of your life if you stick with me. At this moment you are *the* most important dude in vampire history. You're part of the cure and not part of the problem. Give me your arm for a second. It won't hurt, just a little pinch."

Mesmerized by the look in Hobo's eyes, Nickel held out his skinny arm. What the heck, he figured, been on all kinds of trips. Might as well go on this one.

The slight pressure of sharpened fangs pierced the soft skin near Nickel's brachial artery in less time than it took for him to blink. Frightened at first, the cool tingling from Hobo's lips numbed the twin punctures and warm waves of relaxation rolled through his veins. Hobo grabbed one of the copper rings and placed it on his friend's right hand then stood back and admired his handiwork.

Saliva trickled down Nickel's chin and his bloodshot eyes rolled back in his head. He stumbled and almost fell to his knees. The faint blue veins that snaked through his liver-spotted hands deflated second by second and his pale skin, once the color of fresh whipped cream, turned translucent and gray.

"You'll be ok, buddy. Any second now and the jolt will hit you and we'll go hunting together. The first feed is always the best. I'll teach you everything I know and then, when you're ready..."

A loud sound, like the zap of crackling lightning filled the small room. Hobo stared in horror as Nickel's skinny body shuddered, shifted, and swirled until it dissolved into a pile of fiery red ash. The copper ring rolled beneath a piece of oil-stained machinery and Nickel's granny glasses tumbled to the ground shattering on impact.

"Shit!" Hobo screamed."Shit! Shit! Shit!"

CHAPTER THIRTY-NINE

After a tense week of watching, waiting, and hoping for a positive response from Marcus, Jade's phone rang early one morning and her answering machine clicked on. "Jade, it's Marcus. I really need to speak with you. It's Wednesday morning. I'll be at Brim's Diner tonight at 9 p.m. Hope you can meet me there. Thanks."

Jade heard the message and went back to sleep nestled in silken sheets. She arose at dusk and drove directly to Nightshade Manor for a meeting with Lucien, Wolf, and Savanna. "How did he sound?" Savanna asked. "Could you get a feel for what he's thinking?"

"No, can't tell much from a recording but there was no animosity or anger in his voice. I hope we appealed to the healer side of him, the part that feels a responsibility to relieve suffering and help those in need. Guess I won't know till I see him," she shrugged.

A cuckoo clock chimed eight times and Wolf tapped the wooden table with his index fingers. "I don't trust mortals, especially this one. He knows too much. I think we should go with you and stay out of sight just in case things get out of hand. If he makes the wrong decision and tries to expose us we can take appropriate action."

They rose in unison, intent on protecting Jade and The

Vampire Preservation Society. Jade left in her Corvette and the others piled into Lucien's black Hummer.

An arched doorway lined with sparkling bead curtains connected Brim's Diner to a new age bookstore where customers scanned books and magazines and sniffed pastel colored aromatherapy candles to clear their minds and senses. Tarot cards, pentagrams, and rows of rainbow tinted gemstones lined the counter by the register and sticks of fragrant incense stood erect in sand-filled bowls ready to be lit on request. Jade glanced in the local author section to be sure her books were available for purchase and looked around Brim's to see if Marcus had arrived; her friends sat outside behind the dark-tinted windows of Lucien's vehicle.

She spotted him sitting at a table near the floor to ceiling window at the front of the diner. Dark circles smudged his eyes and he seemed troubled, a slight twitching in his hands revealing a nervousness she had never seen before. She strolled to the table and took a seat across from him. "Hi Marcus," she said grabbing his hand. "Good to see you again."

Marcus looked up. It seemed as though he had aged in a few short days. His eyes had the heavy look of someone who hadn't slept but tossed and turned in rumpled sheets as the hours ticked by. He was frazzled and worn out but brightened when Jade touched him.

"Thanks for coming. I've been working day and night, looking at test tubes, microscopes, charts, and computer programs trying to make sense of the blue ash phenomena. I thought at first that you and your friends were joking, but the biological components of the remains you gave me are fascinating and warrant further testing."

A heavyset waitress ambled to the table and handed them menus. "Drinks?" she asked, pen poised to write.

"Sam Adams Boston Lager," Marcus answered. Jade looked at him and smiled.

"Make that two," she added caressing his hand across the table.

Jade was anxious not knowing what the doctor was going to do next. She didn't drink beer but felt it would put Marcus more at ease if she joined him with a brew. The waitress returned with their drinks and they ordered a platter of appetizers to munch on while they continued to chat.

"Marcus, the leaders of your nation raped and killed millions of innocent people throughout the ages yet they are immortalized on your money, in buildings, and in countless ways across the world. I don't understand how greed and ignorance can be held in such high esteem."

Marcus peeled bits of the shiny blue label off his beer bottle and rolled the tiny slivers of paper into small pea sized balls. He sighed and wiped his mouth with the back of his hand. "Jade, humans have done terrible things to each other since cavemen whacked each other with sticks and stones. I can't change history but I can create my own destiny as a healer. I learned at a young age that compassion and pain are intertwined, that you can't fully comprehend the strength of one without experiencing the other. The gateway to anyone's soul is through their heart and the ability to heal isn't learned in a medical book, it's nurtured from within when someone steps outside their comfort zone and shares that wisdom with another."

Jade looked down at her food, a single pink tear sliding down her cheek like a rose petal drifting from a thorny stem. "Does this mean..."

"Yes, it means I'll help you. Your ideas and concerns have merit and I can't let others suffer when I might be able to come up with a solution. I'm waiting for a shipment of some pharmaceutical supplies from overseas then I can resume testing. Let your friends know I'm not the enemy and I will keep you apprised of my progress as I move along."

Jade rose from her chair and wrapped her arms around the weary doctor. She inhaled his scent and felt the lust hunger rise in her throat and press against her lips. She whispered in his ear. "Can't wait to see you again, Marcus. Thank you."

They left at the same time, Marcus heading to his SUV in

the parking lot and Jade to the black Hummer waiting outside.

"It's a go!" she yelled. "Now, let's go eat. I'm starving!"

CHAPTER FORTY

Wolf rested beneath a pile of golden pine needles and tried to quiet the constant buzzing in his head caused by all the activity surrounding the blue ash disease. It became apparent to him after the meeting with Marcus that the only way to find a path to a cure was to use the sacred plant medicines of his ancestors to seek answers to the questions that burned inside his mind.

Ren and Skye's death screams still haunted him and the questions surrounding their deaths remained unanswered yet the crisis continued unabated and he was frustrated by his own inability to do anything about it.

The decision to tap into ancient ways was not an easy one. Altered states of consciousness did not come easy for immortals; their heightened senses already affected their abilities and to go beyond that realm took strength, determination, and stamina. After careful consideration Wolf decided against a peyote ceremony. Chewing small pieces of the sacred cacti would actually diminish its effects because of his accelerated metabolism and he didn't want to disrespect the sanctity of the ceremony. He decided to visit Peru where a sacred visionary brew called *ayahuasca* was said to assist those on spiritual quests. His indigenous cousins recommended an old *ayahuasquero* named Ricardo who would prepare the special mixture of *Psychotria Viridis* and *Banisteriopsis caapi* vine in a secluded spot near a tiny village. Wolf brought an offering of colorful prayer ties filled with tobacco and a large bundle of white sage to honor their shared heritage.

Ricardo stirred a small pot of bubbling brew and waved his hand towards a thatched ceremonial hut. His crinkled brown eyes flashed in his broad brown face and his jet black hair tumbled over his shoulders in thick waves.

"Sit in the *maloca*," he said quietly.

Wolf sat on a mat and looked up at the thatched ceiling of the ceremonial hut. He inhaled the earthy scent of decaying tropical plants and felt the steamy jungle air tickle the insides of his sensitive nostrils. The maloca reminded him of the many sweat lodges he had built out of willow tree branches and heavy blankets. He could almost smell the smoke from sacred pipes filled with kinnikinnick and imagined the sizzling sound of water being poured on heated rocks, steam rising into puffs of silent spirits soothing heavy hearts and mending broken souls. He hoped this ceremony would cleanse his mind and give him a vision of hope for the future of his immortal race.

Ricardo shuffled along the path to the maloca and sat on the ground next to Wolf. He placed a thick hand-rolled cigarette on a small woven cloth next to a bundle of dried leaves called a *chacapa*, a ceremonial rattle used to chase evil spirits away, and then filled a small carved gourd with the *ayahuasca* brew and handed it to Wolf.

"I cannot guide you on your search, brother, but I can help prepare you for your journey. You are the seeker and I am just a signpost on the way to the spirit world. Beware of the *chullachaquis!* They have been known to lead people down the wrong road. I will pray over you in this world and hope that you find answers in the next."

Wolf placed his offerings next to Ricardo's on the cloth and gulped the bitter fluid. Anticipation and excitement flooded his senses like the thrill of a good hunt on a crowded city street. He stretched out on the hard dirt floor and closed his eyes to wait while the brew trickled through the gateways of his immortal mind. Ricardo whistled and shook whispering chacapa leaves over Wolf's body. The sound was soothing, reminding Wolf of swaying palm fronds clattering in a breeze. Next the familiar scent of tobacco smoke curling over his body as Ricardo sang an *icaro,* a healing melody meant to introduce spiritual travelers to the beginning of their journeys.

Wolf felt a gentle tingle behind his eyes that spread throughout his body as each second passed. He sat up and Ricardo handed him a lit candle stuffed into the middle of a smooth wooden disc. The flame from the candle released a torrent of emotions as he relived the last moments of mortality during the other vision quest centuries ago. He placed his trembling hand on his chest, the lub dub of his heartbeat echoing in his ears as he honored the four directions. Pink tears clouded his eyes as he watched the movie screen of his mind, feeling the pain of his dying relatives deep within his soul and reliving those final gasps of mortal breaths as he transitioned into the lonely life of an immortal being.

A hot pink frog caught his attention and led him to a swirling blue meadow filled with shimmering gold flowers and polka dot trees. Two small figures in the distance somersaulted and tap danced along a purple walkway that soon became a slithering speckled snake, mouth agape and silver fangs twinkling like rogue comets blasting through a star-filled sky. One of the dancing imps stood still and stared at Wolf, his beady eyes ricocheting in circles as he jumped from foot to foot. Wolf noticed the creature's gnarled feet; both faced backwards and looked like muddy tree stumps.

A high pitched squeal pierced the air and the little man ran towards the other figure now exiting a lime green teepee filled with broken buffalo skulls. Wolf recognized this one – he was a heyoka, a trickster spirit who did everything backwards. He noticed all the clothing worn turned inside out and the spirit's tangled hair was braided beneath his chin and filled with twigs and crushed acorns. The tiny beings danced back and forth, up and down, and seemed reluctant to do anything else. Nearby the snake's tongue flickered and it dove into the dark depths beneath the psychedelic wonderland and curled around a cracked amethyst geode.

Logical thinking was useless in the spirit world. Any lessons learned were felt and intuited not analyzed or categorized. Wolf's stomach churned, part of his conscious mind recognizing the pangs of hunger that would soon grow stronger. He focused his attention on the two tiny imps and felt a creeping dread lurking in the corners of his mind. They now screeched and grabbed each other's hands, spinning in a circle and drooling gobs of bloody spit. They slowed and skipped like two schoolgirls having fun at recess. Their voices crackled through the air as they sang:

"Ring around our roseys
You are being nosy
Ashes, ashes,
You'll all fall down!"

Startled, Wolf sat up and rubbed his eyes. A bright light beneath his eyelid forced him to shut his eyes. A flashing yellow light hovered over a huge red and white STOP sign and the imps dangled like miniature acrobats swinging on shiny copper rings. A loud bang! A deafening scream! The sign exploded into a pile of blue ash and the copper rings rolled into the gaping jaws of the giant writhing snake.

Wolf stood and grabbed his stomach with trembling hands. Hunger burned in his gut and he fought the urge to bite Ricardo. "Thank you, brother," he croaked. "I found what I needed."

Ricardo bent to pick up his bundle of *chacapa* leaves for a final blessing, but his guest had disappeared.

CHAPTER FORTY-ONE

By day Dr. Marcus Blackwell continued his fundraising activities, networking with specialists from around the world making AIDS research a priority. At night he shifted his focus to the Blues Project, as he referred to it, and met with Jade periodically to give her updates on his work. He transformed his garage from a workshop into a mini-laboratory filled with test tubes, microscopes, slides, books, and automated blood analyzers. A dorm-sized refrigerator held actual blood samples from dying patients and he carefully monitored and replenished the supply when the shelf life expired.

Six months after agreeing to help, Marcus was ready to make an unprecedented announcement. He phoned Jade early one evening and requested a meeting with the others. Her answering machine clicked on as he spoke.

"Hi Jade, I need to speak with everyone as soon as possible. There are some issues we need to address and I'll be leaving next week to attend a conference overseas so time is of the essence, as they say. Call me, please."

Jade listened to the message and called Lucien right away. Together they made a conference call to Savanna and Wolf.

"Jade, any idea what's going on with the good doctor?" Savanna asked.

147

"No, but I know he's been spending most of his nights in his garage working on the Blues Project, as he calls it. He wouldn't ask for a meeting if it weren't important."

Wolf sat beneath a tall saguaro cactus in the Painted Desert of Arizona and checked the reception on his cell phone. The bars flickered up and down each time he moved. "I'm having some problems with my phone. Call me when you set it up." He disconnected and gazed at the sparkling sky over head.

"Lucien, is Wolf okay? He's been even more quiet than usual?" Savanna asked.

Lucien sighed and answered in a thoughtful tone. "He's got a tough job reburying his friends and relatives from years gone by. He could use some quiet time. Back to the request from Blackwell. Where shall we meet? He can't come to Nightshade Manor. The alarm will trigger all kinds of unnecessary panic and our community is under enough pressure as it is. Any ideas?"

Jade doodled on a notepad and considered the options. "We can't go to a restaurant. I don't know what he wants and we certainly can't draw any attention to ourselves if he says something we don't agree with. Savanna, what about the cottage?"

"You're kidding me, right? You know damn well how much I hate those arrogant, self-serving, selfish mortals! I'd do anything for our cause but please don't ask me to contaminate my home with the stench of a cologne drenched, nattering human who has his own twisted agenda for helping us. If you want to fang him, go for it, but find another location."

Jade and Lucien burst out laughing. Savanna's dislike of the human race bordered on comical and they liked to tease her whenever they could.

"He knows where I live," Jade said giggling. "Let's meet here tomorrow night at 10 p.m. and see what he has to say. I'll text Wolf and call Marcus to let him know. I'll pick him up at his condo and that will give me a bit of control over him in case he turns on us."

CHAPTER FORTY-TWO

The headlights from Lucien's Hummer danced on the walls of Jade's living room when he pulled into the driveway. As soon as he and others arrived Jade called Marcus to let him know she was on the way. Her sleek green car hugged the curvy roads like a tendril wrapped around a sturdy stem. Marcus was outside waiting for her, a newspaper in one hand, a can of soda in the other. He smiled when she pulled up to the curb and gently stroked her hand as they headed back to her house.

Tea light candles flickered inside tiny frosted globes as they all took a seat around the living room. A bottle of Perrier water stood out amongst four goblets of crimson blood lining the kitchen counter. Jade placed the drinks on a silver tray and walked around the room. The tension in the room was punctuated with an eerie silence.

Marcus glanced at his watch and began speaking. "Thanks for meeting with me. I'll get right to the point. I've spent the last six months working on the Blues Project in a mini-lab I set up in my garage. I recognize the dire need for answers and solutions. I have good news and bad news, as they say, and there are no easy answers for either side of this equation. The bad news is I need more time to work on your Blues Project. I am juggling a heavy workload both in and out of work and can't keep up this hectic pace. I need a break."

Savanna slapped her hand on the table and yelled. "I knew we couldn't trust a mortal to do a vampire's job. Told all of you this wasn't a good idea but nobody would listen. Now he wants to take off somewhere holding our fate in his hands. Bullshit!"

Lucien interrupted. "Wait Savanna, he's not finished."

Marcus paused and took a deep breath. Beads of sweat trickled down the sides of his smiling face and his hands trembled with excitement.

"The only way to stop the spread of any viral outbreak is to control the source of the outbreak. I believe I've discovered a cure for AIDS and it's derived from *your* blue ash! Once developed and approved, it will change medicine as we know it. The downside is vampires will be hunted for their blood and remains, predators becoming prey, but think of the ramifications! Patients will be cured and the life span of mortals will increase significantly if we can find other uses for the remains. We can eradicate the AIDS virus and your people will benefit by having a more bio-diverse source of food. It's a winning combination from where I sit."

The four vampires sat in stunned silence trying to absorb the news. They each thought of how their mortal lives were ruined by the greediness and callousness of others. Marcus rose from his chair and shook everyone's hand.

"Sorry I have to leave. I have an important call in an hour and need to get home. I'll call a cab..."

"No," Jade said abruptly. "I'll take you."

The three remaining leaders sat morosely, teeth grinding, anger seething below the surface of calm exteriors. Six piercing eyes followed the departing couple as they walked out the door. Lucien grabbed a crystal pitcher of fresh blood and hurled it across the room. Shards of blood stained glass twinkled beneath glowing candles and slid down the pale yellow wall.

"History will NOT repeat itself," he snarled. "We are here to preserve our society, not become preservatives in some greedy pharmaceutical potion! There has got to be another way!"

CHAPTER FORTY-THREE

Thick fog draped the roads like patches of gray gauze on gaping wounds. Jade maneuvered her Vette up rain-slickened roads towards Blackwell's condo. She pulled up to the curb, switched the interior light on, and glared at Marcus.

"I promise I'll keep trying to help you and your friends," Marcus stammered. "This is such a great opportunity. You may not realize it yet but..."

Jade raised her hand to silence him. "Please Marcus, just get out. I can't talk right now. I'll call you tomorrow night after I've calmed down."

Marcus pushed the door open and stepped onto the sidewalk. Jade pealed out, tires screeching and engine revving like a race car warming up for the track. He watched the taillights fade into the thick fog and reached into his jacket pocket for his ring of keys. He jiggled the silver key back and forth in the front door lock cursing himself for forgetting to spray some graphite into the jagged steel slit. A large evergreen bush rustled beside him as the tumblers fell in place releasing the stubborn lock.

"Welcome," a crackling voice whispered. Two fangs pierced the pulsing carotid artery of Blackwell's neck and he crumpled to the ground in a heap. A copper ring clinked softly against the band of his watch as it was placed on his finger and a folded note was tucked into the pocket of his jeans.

Waking an hour later, tangled in twisted sheets, a burning hunger clawed at his insides like fire ants chewing on tender flesh. Jumbled images flickered through his aching head and his sandpaper throat craved moisture each time he swallowed. Craving raw meat, he stumbled to the dimly lit kitchen and yanked on the refrigerator door hoping to quench the blazing fire burning in his veins. A package of blood streaked steak caught his eye and he ripped it open, shredding the raw meat with virgin incisors. The burning sensation was now a glow, the knot in his gut a dull ache of sore muscles and the need for sleep overpowering. He crawled back to bed on plush beige carpeting and grabbed the edge of his nightstand for support. He noticed a folded note tucked beneath his brown leather wallet. He opened it and read: *Healers Can't Be Dealers.*

CHAPTER FORTY-FOUR

Jade's phone rang over and over again like a fire alarm gone awry. Mentally exhausted after the meeting with Marcus, she had slipped out to feed and wanted nothing more than to sleep. The incessant ringing jangled her frayed nerves and she grabbed the phone to check the Caller I.D. It was Marcus but she wasn't ready to talk just yet.

The phone rang again and she grabbed it. "Yes," she grumbled into the receiver.

"Jade! Jade! You're finally home!"

She sat up and brushed her hair out of her eyes.

"Marcus, what's wrong?"

"I was attacked last night!" he croaked.

"Are you hurt? I can't come over during daylight, but I can be there after dusk."

"I'm beyond hurt or injured. I think I've become one of you! Something bit me and the next thing I knew I was in bed and slurping blood off a Styrofoam plate like a rabid dog. Jade, I have fangs!" he screeched.

She stared at the phone as if Marcus would suddenly materialize in front of her. "Are you telling me you've been bit? One of us? Are you sure you didn't have another bad dream? Maybe all the supernatural mumbo-jumbo around here has worked its way into your psyche."

Marcus sobbed into the phone like a starving child. She knew he would need to feed soon. "Marcus, call in sick. You need to clear your calendar for a few days. Things will get worse if we don't deal with this right away."

"How can they things get any worse!" he yelled. "I've had a major scientific breakthrough and I can't do anything about it. Do you realize what this means? I can't reveal my findings. I'll be hunted down like the rest of you!"

"Marcus, stay indoors and get some rest. You'll need your strength later on. I'll be over at sunset."

Jade watched the sun dissolve into an ashen horizon. She called Lucien to let him know she was coming and raced towards Nightshade Manor. She scanned her ring and hurried to the meeting room where Lucien sat reading a book by firelight.

"Hello my friend," he said without looking up. "To what do I owe…"

"Marcus has been turned!" she blurted out. "He's furious and famished and I'm on my way to see him."

Marcus closed his book. "An interesting turn of events," he said dryly. "Does he know who sired him?"

She shook her head. "I'm going to take him to Boston and help him acclimate. He needs some guidance and I want to be sure he's not going to be a danger to himself or us for that matter."

"I'll let the others know."

Lucien felt a gnawing fear in his gut. Things were out of control and there was too much at stake for anyone to be complacent. He walked to his desk and made to conference call to Wolf and Savanna. They answered at the same time.

"Lucien, what's up?" Wolf asked.

"Hi Lucien," Savanna yawned.

"Is he boring you already?" Wolf chuckled.

"This is anything but boring. Either one of you munch on a McMarcus meal last night?" Lucien asked.

"What are you talking about?" Savanna answered.

"Our doctor friend was re-born to the dark side last night

155

according to Jade, and is out for blood in more ways than one."

The line was silent for a few seconds. "It wasn't us Lucien," Wolf said slowly. "Savanna and I were at a heavy metal concert in Foxboro hunting in the parking lots while the band jammed."

Savanna giggled. "There's something to be said for loud music, moshing mortals, and adrenaline laced blood. So what do we do now with Dr. Hypocrite?"

"Jade is handling Blackwell tonight and will meet with us tomorrow night at midnight. This may work to our advantage in the long run. He'll be more inclined to search for *our* cure now that he's one of us. Let's see what Jade has to say tomorrow, and in the meantime, stay safe and sated."

CHAPTER FORTY-FIVE

J ade cruised down the street and noticed a hunched body crouching beneath a bush outside of Blackwell's condo. She beeped and the shadowy figure appeared at the passenger side window pounding and wailing in desperation.

"Quick I can't let anyone see me like this," Marcus pleaded.

She pushed a button and the door flew open revealing a disheveled, pale Marcus. They rode in silence for several minutes, Marcus peering through the windows like a prisoner released from jail. Jade handed him a bottle of Hemo-Sip and spoke softly.

"Drink that. It will help with the pain."

He raised the bottle to his mouth, repulsed by his actions but left with no other options. The crimson fluid coated his throat like fine cognac on a summer eve. His mouth tingled and his gums ached slightly as he finished the whole bottle.

He closed his eyes and listened to the conversations of families tucking their children into bed. The scent of sweet hay and pine trees tickled his nostrils, and the sky was an explosion of fireworks, a canvas of celestial beauty.

"Marcus, are you okay?" Jade asked softly as she drove south towards Boston.

"It's incredible," he whispered. "There's a whole new universe out there."

"You're going to love this. Ever been to a rave doc?" she asked handing him a Red Sox cap and a pair of Ray Ban glasses.

He jerked backwards, spasms of pain rippling down his arms and legs. "No I haven't. What's wrong with me?" he snapped. "Why do I hurt like this?"

"You need to feed," she answered matter-of-factly. "We're here. Just follow my lead and stay close."

The club pulsed with flashing strobe lights and pounding techno music. Fluorescent bodies jerked up and down like schools of neon fish gasping for air and bottles of water floated through the crowd like bubbles of pink champagne careening in a sparkling glass.

Marcus stood, transfixed by all the sensory input and overwhelmed by the chaotic energies. Jade reached out and took his hand.

"It's called Dub step. The kids are listening for a distinctive downbeat and choreograph their moves to the bass. We're safe here. Some of these kids are on Ecstasy and feel invincible because of their elevated serotonin levels. There defenses are down and it's all about the love. Makes it easier to feed. C'mon, I'll show you."

Marcus watched Jade sashay out onto the dance floor and mingle with the mass of sweaty dancers. Her sequined dress sparkled like hundreds of prisms strung in sun-drenched windows and her emerald eyes glowed like a laser beam searching for a target. She settled on a young man with a bright orange Mohawk and pierced eyebrows. She whispered something into his ear and motioned for Marcus to follow.

Outside in the darkened alley the music echoed between the graffiti covered walls. Jade giggled, pulling the terrified morsel towards her ripping his shirt away from his throat to expose the pulsing arteries. She bit the soft flesh and grabbed Marcus by the nape of his neck and shoved his mouth onto the dripping wound.

"Drink," she commanded.

He placed his quivering lips on the two small holes and felt the warm coppery fluid trickle into his parched throat. Any disgust he felt melted away as his veins filled with the nourishment he so desperately needed and he squeezed the boy's neck to make the blood flow faster. He stopped when his gut was full and gently placed the limp body on the ground.

"Let's go," Jade said yanking him towards the car. "It'll get easier as time goes on. I wanted you to see how easy it is to hunt in crowds where no one pays any attention to what you're doing."

Marcus opened the door and sat in his seat, shoulders slumped, head hung low. He passed the initiation into immortality but felt no joy whatsoever.

CHAPTER FORTY-SIX

The next night the four weary leaders met at the castle. Lucien filled a table with refreshments and called the meeting to order.

"Once again we meet under serious circumstances," he began.

"Serious?" Savanna exclaimed. "Quite frankly, I'm relieved! We're safe. The good doctor can't possibly expose or exploit us without risking his own life and he can't do anything with his current research. I'd say this is a win-win."

Wolf looked up from the flaming logs in the fireplace and shook his head. "Savanna, we can't underestimate our neo-nemesis. He is a healer by nature. Books and schools didn't teach him how to care, it is an inherent quality of his soul and we cannot presume he'll lose that trait because he's reborn. He has our money and at this point, I'm pretty wary of him."

Lucien nodded in agreement. "Savanna I understand your reasoning and appreciate your candor, but like Wolf, I feel Blackwell is unpredictable at this juncture. Perhaps Jade can give us some insight into his state of mind. She has, after all, introduced him to the fine art of feeding."

The group chuckled and broke some of the tension in the room. Jade cleared her throat and stood near the door. "It's hard to know where to start. Marcus is despondent and not quite resigned to his new life. His first feed was a success. I was able to provide him with a live meal but I was afraid he was going to throw himself out of the car on the way home. I'm guessing it dawned on him that rolling around in the middle of a busy highway would do no good since he's now immortal."

Savanna stood and stretched her arms over her head."I think you're all making a mountain out of a molehill as stupid humans say. Let's wait, see what happens, and then deal with whatever developments come our way."

"Okay," Wolf agreed. "He's willing to confide in Jade and I trust her judgment. Let's meet back here on the next full moon – give him time to assimilate. Jade can monitor his activities while keeping up with her own projects and the rest of us can do the same. I'm off to Magdalena, New Mexico, to check on some bones. See you soon."

They toasted each other and scattered in different directions, determined to work towards their survival.

Savanna hurried home, changed into a pair of navy blue yoga pants and matching tee shirt, and called Lucas. His answering machine clicked on. "Lucas, call me as soon as you get this message. I've got some interesting news, a new chapter to add to our on-going mystery. Talk to you later."

She drove into town, grabbed some drafting supplies, and returned home after feeding to consider the new development. She wondered if Blackwell would turn renegade and go off by himself or if he would reveal the cure to mortals and help save their lives. Deep in thought, she didn't notice the crunch of gravel behind her until a hand rested on her shoulder and a familiar voice whispered in her ear.

"Good evening Ms. Martin. I'm returning your call, in person. I hope you don't mind."

She smiled and pushed the door open. "Not at all, Mr. LaPierre, not at all. We have a lot to catch up on and your timing is perfect. Please come in and make yourself at home. Care for some Hemo-Sip?"

"Sounds good. Nice place you've got here."

"Thanks," she said filling two maroon goblets with artificial blood. She handed him his drink and sat next to him on the couch. "Marcus, the mortal magician, used our money and changed the mission into a personal agenda of his own. Lo and behold, he has found a cure for AIDS and you'll never guess what it is."

Lucas looked at her and shook his head. "What do you mean a cure for AIDS? Who cares about mortal medicine? Don't tell me he double-crossed my brother and took off with the money!"

Savanna sipped her drink and peered at him behind dark lashes. "He didn't take the money, but maybe he should have run from us. Blackwell's discovery is that our blue ash can be used to cure AIDS, cancer, and who knows what else, but there's a delicious twist to the story that I'm sure you'll appreciate. He is now the newest member of the Vampire Preservation Society! Someone sired him last night, and according to Jade, he's mad as hell."

They both burst out laughing, pink tears racing down their cheeks till they wore themselves out enjoying the irony of it all.

Upstairs in her room a clock chimed six times and daylight peeked over the horizon. "It's that time," Savanna said yawning into her hand.

Lucas placed his hand on her knee and looked into her eyes. "Got room for another cold body in your bed? I don't want to impose, mind you, but we can continue our discussion when we wake up like mortal companions do." He chuckled at the mortal reference knowing how much she hated the inferior race.

"C'mon up," she said grabbing him by the hand and leading him upstairs. "I've got the perfect place for you to rest your weary fangs."

CHAPTER FORTY-SEVEN

For several weeks Marcus refused to speak to anyone. His door remained locked, windows shuttered against daylight, and his answering machine blinked red with a tape full of messages. Between book signings and conferences Jade secretly watched him, peeking through the garage door where he worked each night until dawn, hidden from the world and nosy neighbors. It appeared he was keeping his promise to help them and she felt a sense of relief each time she saw slivers of fluorescent light beam from behind closed blinds.

One night when the horizon burst into shades of pastel pink, orange, and yellow, Marcus decided to take a stroll to some small shops near his home. The air felt like cool silk pressed against his face and pungent smells assaulted his nose. He stopped for a few moments, closing his eyes and focusing on each scent as if he were a perfumer testing a new fragrance. His nostrils twitched slightly and he was able to separate the harsh synthetic odors of man-made pollutants from the sweet smells of growing green grass and budding trees.

His eyes burned slightly when he got too close to humans. The stench of strong colognes and aftershave felt like flames in his nostrils and he wiped his nose with his sleeve. Older people smelled like fading flowers that lost their bloom and younger ones smelled like scented laundry detergents and cheap soap.

Two lovers strolled ahead of him, arms around each other, oblivious to him and the rest of the world. He watched them for several minutes, and then averted his eyes, feeling like an intruder. He wiped something off his cheeks, surprised to see pink-tinged tears glistening on his finger tips. He truly missed his mortal life but longed for Jade's company even more.

He walked back home and drove to the town library, spending about an hour inside the New Age aisle, leaving with a pile of books tucked under his arm and a grin on his flushed face.

After settling on his couch with a glass of Hemo-Sip and a bright yellow highlighter, Marcus picked up the phone and called Jade.

"Hi Jade. Hope you're doing well. I've been pretty busy and thought we could get together at my place tomorrow night about nine. If you can't make it let me know, otherwise I look forward to seeing you."

One of the advantages of enhanced vision that Marcus enjoyed was the ability to speed read vast volumes of work in a short period of time. He spent the night reading and taking notes to prepare for his visit with Jade. At nine the following night he heard a rap on his door and smiled.

"Welcome," he said with a sweeping gesture. "It's been too long. Please make yourself comfortable."

Jade sat on a brown striped sofa and glanced at the sun-dappled landscape photos hanging on the walls. "Those are beautiful Marcus. Did you take them?"

Fighting back a rush of emotions, he cleared his throat and walked over to the collection of frames. "This one is from Moab, Utah, the cinematic backdrop for many westerns, and this is Chaco Canyon in New Mexico. The rolling plains and wild horses of South Dakota is one of my favorites. I waited hours for the sun to be in just the right spot and snapped each scene as the light faded throughout the day. The

164

shadows became doorways to new vistas and as they changed, so did my appreciation for their natural beauty. I'll miss that more than anything else I think. Daylight, sunshine, and my cameras, all part of my past."

Jade watched him, playing with her ankh shaped necklace to disguise her growing sense of sadness. Marcus realized he was making her uncomfortable and sat down beside her.

"Been reading a lot," he said pointing to the pile of library books. "Did you know that according to folklore, a dead woman named Mercy Brown supposedly roamed around Rhode Island looking for her family and the townspeople were so scared they exhumed her body, cut out her heart, and then burned it to get rid of the curse?"

Jade laughed and rolled her eyes. "Leave it mortals to make up strange tales."

"Did you know that in ancient China, you, I mean we, were called *kiang shi* and in ancient Peru we were known as *canchus?* And how about this? A how–to manual for vampire prevention says to bury bodies face down, put garlic in the corpse, scatter seeds for distracting demons, and pile heavy rocks on the grave so no one can escape! The list goes on and on. Decapitation, cremation, sunlight, all remedies for the so-called walking dead."

Jade thumbed through one of the books and looked at Marcus. "You know, neither of us asked for immortality and we can't change our circumstances. Vampires deserve compassion and understanding, too. Humans aren't necessarily the highest rung on the evolutionary ladder and they continue to destroy everything around them, including each other. So consider that if you continue your studies."

Marcus took her hand and kissed her gently on the cheek. He wasn't sure if there were any taboos against vampire romance and wasn't ready to find out.

"Thanks for all your help with this. Guess my new reality is some sort of paranormal universe where regular rules don't apply. I need to work within a different set of parameters and remind myself that I can still contribute to a greater sense of purpose in my immortal life."

Jade nodded and placed her other hand on top of his. "I've got to go, Marcus. Keep up the good work and watch your blood levels. I'll be in touch."

CHAPTER FORTY-EIGHT

A year had passed and it was time once again for the annual Vampire Preservation Society meeting at Nightshade Manor. Marcus continued to work on the Blues Project in his garage and everyone else settled into their work routines agreeing to meet once a month for updates.

Lucien decided to throw a surprise birthday party for his brother under the pretense of having a special meeting to thank everyone for their continued efforts in monitoring blue ash fatalities. He called the other leaders sharing his plan extending special invitations to both Marcus and Hobo who hadn't met each other or his older twin. He felt it was time for all team members to get to know each other and a party was a great way to show his appreciation for everyone's hard work.

Hobo was thrilled to finally receive his first invitation to a special meeting at Nightshade Manor, strutting around the outskirts of town like a celebrity on a game show. His copper ring experiment had failed but he was determined to find a way to impress everyone with his genius idea, especially Lucien. The precious doctor won't be able to top me he thought, packing a contaminated ring and a small vial of blue ash into a small canvas bag. I deserve credit for trying to save everyone.

Across town Marcus paced back and forth in his garage,

gathering notes and a printout for the birthday celebration. His gift to the brothers was secret, even Jade had no idea what his plans were. They had dined together the night before on a starlit beach near Cape Cod and as she helped him navigate the complexities of immortal life his self-confidence blossomed and so did his fondness for her. She'll be here soon he mused, and we'll all be celebrating in a big way.

Meanwhile, Savanna ran a chamois cloth over the hood over her Shelby GT 500 and smiled. She would be picking up the birthday cake soon and Lucas had no idea of the feast his twin had planned. The two of them spent many days together cuddled in her armoire, safe from the sun and other intrusions. She promised Lucien she would delay their arrival by a half hour to be sure the others had arrived.

Wolf felt a tingle of apprehension crawl up his spine adding to his sense of wariness as he prepared to walk to the surprise party. Since his plant journey he had become more reflective about his life, both mortal and immortal, and, during frustrating times, was able to strengthen his resolve to preserve and honor his Native culture and way of life. Lately he couldn't help but feel that he was missing something, a detail or hint about communal survival and the quest for a remedy to the blue ash plague.

The sun hung low in a tangerine sky and a gentle ocean breeze drifted through the trees hugging the small patio outside. The small group of friends waited for Lucien to surprise his brother, sipping warm imported blood from engraved thermal mugs and sharing their latest projects. Hobo hadn't made an appearance yet and Lucien secretly hoped he wouldn't.

Lucien stood, tears glistening bloodshot eyes, his drink raised up in the air. "I propose a birthday toast to my twin, Lucas LaPierre, who means more to me than immortality itself. We are reunited once again, sharing the same blood, in more ways than one, and loving each other as only twins can. Happy Birthday Lucas, I am so happy to have you back in my life!"

Everyone clapped and Lucas embraced his younger twin and raised his drink up in the air to salute the others. "I've learned over the centuries that sometimes less is more, that solitude keeps you sane, and that being judged by others has no value and serves no purpose in life other than boosting troubled egos searching for conditional acceptance. Thank you for welcoming me into your lives and for all your good wishes. And to my brother – two halves make a whole and we are now one."

The whole group was moved to tears by the brothers' emotional toasts and the room was quiet for a moment.

Lucas sat next to Savanna and listened to the updates in everyone's lives. Lucien threw a log on the fireplace and asked Wolf about his latest consultation.

"I've been working with the Cherokee Nation helping them chase pot hunters robbing some burial grounds in Georgia. They sneak around at night thinking no one can see them and I jump up out of the ground and scare the shit out of them! Trust me, they don't come back," he said laughing with everyone else.

"Savanna, what have you been up to?" Lucien asked.

She rested her hand on Lucas's knee and smiled. "I've been socializing a bit more," she said coyly, "and I'm working on a geodesic dome project for a client in Arizona. He wants a straw bale, passive solar unit with a wood burning stove for winter and mud walls to keep it cool in summer. We're working online at night. Told him I'm allergic to the sun and I'm as fragile as tumbleweed caught in a dust devil storm and he hasn't asked any questions since."

Everyone laughed and Lucien looked at Jade. "Working on anything new and exciting, Ms. Author?"

Jade stood and reached for a refill. "As a matter of fact I am," she grinned. "I'm on the final draft of my next novel called *The Vampire Preservation Society* and it is guaranteed to become a best seller! A group of friends get together and..."

Savanna jumped up nearly spilling her drink on Lucas. "Are you out of your mind? Writing about us?" she yelled. "What the hell are you thinking – or are you thinking at all?"

Jade stood and faced her friend. "You didn't let me finish! The story follows five Goths who..."

Marcus jumped up out of his chair, unable to contain himself any longer. "Before you two get into a squabble I have an announcement to make."

Surprised at his outburst, Jade and Savanna sat back down and looked at each other, eyebrows raised and lips pursed as if to stifle any escaping sounds.

"As you may or may not know, I was forced to join your exclusive club months ago, against my will, without my consent. I've tried very hard to make the best of the situation, difficult at first, but easier as time went on with Jade's help. I've immersed myself in your culture, participated in many discussions, and continued to work on the Blues Project whenever my schedule allowed. I am very proud to announce that my hard work has paid off! My birthday gift to the illustrious LaPierre brothers is a revolutionary formula using components of the AIDS virus, which is technically an immortal cell, and molecules of blue ash. Blended all together in a proprietary blend it is the cure for vampirism! No more hiding! No more blood! No more darkness!" He looked around the room expecting a joyous reaction, seeing stunned faces and glaring hate-filled eyes.

Lucien stood, anger growing like molten lava ready to spew from a bursting volcano. He grabbed Marcus by the throat and held him against the wall. Jade screamed and Wolf ran to her side to quiet and comfort her.

"You traitorous fool!" Lucien thundered. "Your formula is useless. You can't become mortal again. None of us can. Without vampires you have no blue ash. With no blue ash you have no cure. Your magic potion is worthless and so are you!"

No one spoke. It was as if each one of them had been pulled under the ocean to drown in silent pain.

Lucas grabbed his brother's arm and took him outside to the patio to calm him down. As they huddled together near swaying trees, Hobo traipsed through the nearby woods munching on the remains of a feral cat. He removed the starched white napkin from the tip of his walking stick and wiped his bloody fangs. Off in the distance two muffled voices drifted on the wind and although he couldn't hear any words, he could tell the tone was serious, maybe even threatening, and he hurried toward the castle to get a better look.

Hobo recognized Lucien right away and was troubled by the angry expression on his face and the look in his eyes. He couldn't see the other man's face but caught the glint of a copper earring in the light from the room inside. Got to be that doctor wearing an earring instead of a ring, thinking he's better than everyone else he thought. Must be a hell of an argument, never seen the boss so upset. He's my only friend. I've got to protect Lucien from this quack before things get out of hand. He reached into his bag, grabbing a small packet of powdery blue ash then spit on the tip of his beloved walking stick before dipping it into the ash.

Crashing waves pounded the rocks on the side of the cliff near the patio and Lucas and Lucien continued to talk. Neither one of them saw or heard the poisoned walking stick hurtling through the air. Hobo aimed for the man wearing the copper earring and pierced the target's chest like an over ripe watermelon tossed from a moving truck.

Lucas shrieked, the ungodly sound of a dying vampire drowning out any other sound for miles around. Lucien scooped his brother into his arms and held him close as he dissolved into a heap of ash. Wolf, Jade, and Savanna ran to Lucas's side and screamed at what they saw, clawing at Lucas's clothing as if he could somehow come back to life.

Hobo stood at the edge of the patio, horrified by what he had done. "I didn't mean, I thought it was..." he stammered.

Wolf glanced up and growled, hatred oozing from every pore, sorrow flooding his mind. He picked up the walking stick and impaled Hobo through the heart. He, too, crumpled into ash, his remains swept away in a heavy ocean wind.

Lucien sat on the cold damp ground clutching his brother's

copper ring; numb with grief, a hollow feeling deep inside crushing his mind and strangling his senses.

"Where the hell is Marcus and Jade?" Savanna bellowed. "It's his fault this all happened!" She ran inside and looked around. Wolf checked the driveway and surrounding roads.

"They're gone," he said through clenched teeth. "We've got two fugitives on the run and no way to track them if they return to a mortal life. We've got to regroup and come up with a plan. This is a disaster."

THE END

C olleen J. Pallamary is the author of ***Scammunition : How To Protect Yourself From Con Artists: A Guide For Baby Boomers And Beyond*** and has been working on scam prevention issues for over a decade. She speaks frequently to community groups and writes monthly scam awareness features on her website and social media. She is an AHA Certified CPR/First Aid Instructor, an Extra Class Ham Radio Operator, and has an Honorary Doctorate in Metaphysics Degree.

The Vampire Preservation Society is her first novel. Upcoming projects include ***Black and Blue: An Inside View***, a non-fiction book based on a domestic violence awareness program for female inmates that she developed and taught for several years, and continued research into the scam phenomena.

For more information visit **www.colleenpallamary.com**.

COLLEEN J. PALLAMARY

www.ingramcontent.com/pod-product-compliance
Lightning Source LLC
Chambersburg PA
CBHW071244130626
46556CB00003B/1161